'Lies,' he whispered. 'Lies – it doesn't exist, it isn't here, it never was, it's nothing but a –' He stared up at the blue sky where creatures silently hovered, watching him. 'Lies!' he shouted. *'Lies!'*

Over him, the sky split with a horrible drawn-out scream that filled the world, shaking it, tearing it to pieces. Darkness poured down, then light. The buildings disappeared, swallowed by the screaming ground. The ground heaved and shook, twisting itself into new forms. Monteyiller caught a glimpse of Cat, standing amid the collapsing buildings, staring at him with large disbelieving eyes, her face frozen into immobility. He started to run. The sky crashed down over Anycity, obliterating it.

Sam J. Lundwall

ALICE'S WORLD

ARROW BOOKS

Arrow Books Limited
3 Fitzroy Square, London W1

An imprint of the Hutchinson Publishing Group

London Melbourne Sydney Auckland
Wellington Johannesburg Cape Town
and agencies throughout the world

First published in Great Britain by Arrow Books Ltd 1975
© Sam J. Lundwall 1971

Printed in Great Britain by
Flarepath Printers Ltd, St Albans, Herts

ISBN 0 09 910030 4

1

Already in the early morning, the white stallion had walked the winding path up to the ridge of the mountain. It was a hot day, but he stood there, unmoving, because he had the vague notion that this was expected of him. Beneath him, the ground steamed in the heat, and the creatures down there moved uneasily while they waited for him to give the long-awaited sign; but not until the evening did the event happen that the old women had prophesied. Suddenly the spaceships hung in the sky, like a swarm of flies. They hovered as drops of molten metal in the blue evening light.

Forced by his terrible longing, the stallion strained his muscles and hurled himself out in the air. The mighty white wings spread out from his shoulders and lifted him without visible effort up toward the darkening sky. He swept majestically around the mountain, followed by a thousand watching eyes, and soared with powerful wingbeats out over the endless steel-blue sea, toward the spaceships that danced in the hot evening light far away. Behind him a cloud of flying creatures rose in the air, driven by the same compelling yearning that drove him. There came the Valkyries on their flying horses, the Phoenix, the Sphinx; a colossal man who came from a distant place called Thrudvang and traveled in a flying chariot drawn by two male goats; thousands and thousands of creatures who rushed forward high above the earth. Above them all, Medea raged in a golden coach drawn by dragons, with Oistros as coachman; and following the big swarm came a largish beetle who had relinquished the evening star Venus Mechanitis to its fate. The beetle's name was Khepre, and its nature was the same as the other creatures. But ahead of them all, the Pegasus soared over the sea, toward the sinking ships. The white mane flowed in the wind, and the air thundered with beats from the mighty wings. The Pegasus soared high above the sea that once was called the Mediterranean, toward the distant islands where the returning men's ships would land.

2

The first ship plummeted down from the billowing sky in a wide curve, over the mountaintops and the dark forests, and sank down to the ground. It descended in wide circles, silent as a drifting feather. The long iridescent wings that gave the ship an appearance of a dragonfly pulsed with light and spread a strange shimmer over the ground. The ship glided down between two crumbling pylons of a metal that once had been blinding white but now was dark and lusterless and covered with fissures where dark green vegetation patiently ate its way in; did a turn over a metal launching platform, rusted and fractured by ancient trees, and landed noiselessly. The slender craft, an unlimited expanse of unbroken black metal, hovered unmovingly one foot over the ground, suspiciously watched by the ships above. The pulsating force-fields that had spread out like wings from the black body of the ship faded away and disappeared.

It was a fine evening, cool and quiet and very, very peaceful.

Inside the ship: there were two men fiddling with controls. There were sounds of heavy machinery and the smell of metal and clear oil. A woman dressed in flowing blue stood by the airlock, which opened with a soft soughing sound. She turned around.

'Well?' she asked.

'Well, nothing.' The man had a hard mouth and vacant eyes. 'It's dead. So what do you expect? A welcoming committee?' His voice was high-pitched, contrasting strangely with his burly body.

'It's so . . . different from what I expected,' she said, looking out in the dusk. She clasped and unclasped her hands on her back; her hair spilled down black; there was a vague scent of *Styrax calamitus*.

'You know, Jocelyn,' she said, 'just – something.'

'Sure.' The high-pitched voice.

The other man, seated in the maneuver chair by the shimmering visor screen, didn't say anything. He leaned back, hands loose in his lap, eyes closed, a smile on his mouth. His skin, in the wavering light from the screen, had an odd quality. Jocelyn rose slowly from his chair. 'Let's go,' he said.

Outside: It once had been one of Earth's biggest spaceports – but that was fifty thousand years ago. Now it was a wilderness of moldering structures where mighty trees triumphantly rose from the uneven ground. Remnants of machines and vehicles lay scattered everywhere. A feeling of decay hung over the place, so thick one could almost smell it. Far away in the dusk one could vaguely make out the crumbling remnants of something that might have been an ancient spaceship. It was incredibly large, the naked beams protruded from the hull like the ribs of a giant, blackened corpse.

Jocelyn and Martha appeared in the airlock, momentarily outlined against the blue-white light in the ship, before they jumped down. The ground was weathered and brittle and crunched beneath their weight. As they walked away from the ship, openings appeared in the hull, and rods and barrels slid out, locking into position with soft, well-oiled clicks. The gleaming metal, humming with power, scanned the surroundings with precise, mechanical movements. There was beauty in the movements, and death.

Martha looked up. She threw out her arms, her eyes widening.

'Look!' she whispered. *'Look!'*

The landscape changed. The moldering structures flowed and shimmered, growing, transforming. Ruins rose up toward the sky, changing, hardening into stone and crystal; pillars

8

appeared, their surfaces rippling with liquid fire, reaching up and up toward immense arches of petrified light, ringing with the sound of distant bells. The air hardened into emeralds and rubies, sparkling with light, adorning the majestic walls. The ground changed and became an immense stone-paved floor, reaching away into a misty distance; dark massive structures rose, towering above them; the moon changed, splitting into a thousand flickering candles burning beneath the great arches; there was the sound of an immense choir, whispering clearly and singing. Enormous arched windows appeared, the stained glass alive with dazzling light; there were ornaments and sculptures, and impossibly high up in the blue distance of the arches, there were figures moving. It was the cathedral of Rheims, but a hundred times, a thousand times. It rose on and on, never ending, the altar shrouded in billowing mists, the walls burning with the colors of crystals. The ship was a speck of dust resting in the nave between glowing pillars reaching up into eternity. There was the sound of a chime and someone stood in the pulpit, turning the pages of an immense book decorated with strange signs. The voice boomed out, echoing between walls and pillars and ogival arches, carried on the shoulders of the whispering choir, filling the immense expanse of the cathedral.

Jocelyn threw his hands before his eyes and screamed; and by the terrible fear of the cry the immense voice faltered, the choir became silent. The high-pitched scream filled the cathedral, shaking it. The pillars trembled, the arched windows lost their color, the sculptures melted away. Crystal fell, disintegrating into flashing fragments; the ground heaved, the walls flowed back, shrinking and disappearing in thin wisps of glittering air.

The cathedral collapsed silently, turning into smoke and air. After a moment, nothing was left except for a distant echo of chimes, slowly dying out in the wind.

The man in the ship focused his eyes on the screen before him. The ruins returned, brooding in the pale light of the moon, and in a dark doorway, flanked by crumbling pillars of dark green stone, stood a small girl. She could have been about ten years old, in a bright blue dress, white stockings and a newly-starched pinafore. Her hair was yellow and long, falling down her back; she was bouncing a gaily colored ball up and down on the rubble-strewn ground, looking at the ship with mischievously glinting eyes and shaking with suppressed laughter.

The man regarded the screen with cold, impassive eyes for a while, then abruptly disconnected the camera and swiveled the chair around. He looked thoughtfully at the dials, still registering the unbelievable mass that had surrounded the ship, coming from nowhere and departing again. Had he been anyone else, he would have whistled; but of course, he wasn't. In the merciless blue light of the meter console, the smooth flesh-colored oval of his face was clearly revealed, featureless except for the large unblinking eyes and the delicate round mouth. It was an orthodox arrangement, to be sure, but, then, people prefer their robots as human as possible. He threw a couple of switches and connected unhurriedly with the flagship, hovering somewhere above. A mirage, probably, or a hallucination. He leaned back in the chair as the image of a uniformed man slowly appeared on the screen. There was nothing unusual in hallucinations. But on the other hand, even if human beings can experience hallucinations, robots never do.

3

'But he did!' Monteyiller said. He was a big, stout man dressed in a simple blue tunic with the spaceship-and-sun sign embroidered on the left breast. His eyes, under the mass of unruly black hair, were narrowed, his nose large and aquiline, the mouth determined. He leaned over the table, passing his eyes over the people in the room. 'He saw it,' he said, 'and the instruments bear him out.' He hesitated. 'Some of them, anyway. Now, what kind of hallucination would do that, I ask you?'

Edy Burr, one of the computer specialists, looked up. He said, 'You want my professional opinion?'

'Well, of course.'

'In that case, I haven't got any. I handle the computers, they're good things, mostly, logical and all that. I fed in the information about this . . . occurrence. . . .' His voice trailed off.

'Yes?'

'As far as the computers are concerned,' Edy said, 'it was a hallucination. I got some very good proof, too.'

'I wish I had your simple faith in your computers,' Monteyiller said. 'Unfortunately, I don't.'

'Hallucinations can happen,' said Catherine diRazt, the psychologist. 'Especially under stress. Jocelyn and Martha were quite wound up, weren't they?'

'Sure.' He smiled joylessly at her. 'And the robot as well, perhaps? And the instruments?' He straightened up and went around the table, to the visor screen that covered one of the walls of the room. 'And the television system as well, I gather!' He shook his head. 'What kind of hallucinations can be seen on a visor screen, I ask you.'

'Mirages . . .' Edy said, uncertainly.

'Mirages, my ass! The mass meters nearly jumped off their pins when that . . . thing appeared. Just appeared out of nothing and then disappeared again. Now, what kind of hallucination is that?'

'A cathedral,' someone said, 'early Gothic, I would guess. Very impressive architecture.'

'Thanks,' Monteyiller snapped, 'for nothing. Look, I don't care if it was a fairy castle standing upside-down. I want to know where it came from and how; that's all I'm interested in. And don't tell me what the computers say, because I don't care about that either. Any ideas?'

None. Monteyiller raised his eyebrows, shrugged and turned to the visor screen. Pictures blazed forth there, pictures of heavily surging waters, forests, jungles, endless savannahs where half-sentient creatures roamed beneath the scorching sun, snow-covered wastes, mountains, valleys, deserts, seas. And ruins. From the fourteen dragonfly-ships that circled the planet, telescopic cameras tirelessly watched the landscape and transmitted a never-ending stream of pictures to the ships. The pictures alternated continuously, but the result was the same. At the poles, the ice had swallowed the cities and strange white beasts patrolled the wastes where once the spires and pylons of an incredible civilization had soared toward the limitless sky. The jungles had covered cities and spaceports with an impenetrable covering of fermenting verdure; the glittering spires had fallen beneath the ancient giant tree's roots; and in the former parade halls the apes presided in a pitiable parody of the Imperial rulers' pompous court. On the beaches, on the plains and in the mountains, the cities lay wrecked and crumbled down to dust. Everything was dilapidated, forgotten and defiled. A thousand years from now, nothing would be left of Man's achievements. It was a pitiable sight, but not wholly unexpected.

'I wonder what we had been expecting,' he muttered look-

12

ing at the screen. 'A developed civilization, perhaps . . . the old Empire still going strong and giving the big welcome to the lost son. . . . It doesn't exactly look promising.' He frowned, and turned around. 'Okay,' he said, 'that's all. Try to come up with something, anything at all. But make it fast.'

The room emptied amid a murmur of dissenting voices, abruptly cut off by the closing door. Monteyiller gazed vacantly after them, lost in his own thoughts. He felt old and tired, the skin on his face was dry and rough, and weariness washed over him like waves on a slowly surging sea.

Someone moved in the room. He looked up and met the eyes of Catherine diRazt, standing by the table. 'So you're staying, Cat? Just like old times, isn't it?' He smiled. 'Always the good samaritan, giving consolation to anyone in need. Or perhaps you have some ideas?'

'You know I haven't.'

'Consolation, then.' He leaned back, clasping his hands behind his head. 'You know, for a moment I thought you had something else. Any good, uncomplicated explanation would do.' He looked thoughtfully at her. 'You think it was a hallucination?'

'No.'

'Neither do I. And, you know, it scared the living hell out of me. What's going on here?'

She sat up on the table, tucking her legs under her in the familiar way he knew so well. There was a world of memories in her movements, the hint of unspoken words, the volumes of questions and answers in a raised eyebrow, an inclined head, a closed mouth, a quick gesture with a hand. The lithe body beneath the blue tunic, bearer of no secrets, the long graceful hands that had caressed him so many times. Yes, him. He looked up into her eyes.

She's pitying me! he thought. *It's all the same, pitying, and the kind words and the kind deeds, damnit! That's the perfect psychologist for you, but she was born that way, with a confessional in her head. The compassionate, passionate.*

Suddenly, he longed for her.

13

Years back: They had been a good, reliable scout team, thrown together by a computer's whim and sent out to months of togetherness. Two months in a ten-by-ten foot cabin makes lovers even of strangers. Bodies joining in hate, if not in love. Fighting boredom with lust: and they had managed. They had managed.

They had preceded the fleets of the growing Confederation of Planets, riding the currents of space in their diminutive scoutship, homing in on the dead planets of the dead Empire where ancient splendor lay moldering under alien suns, the sepulchers of Man, scattered over the eternity of space. There had been dead cities, dead memories, dead glory, blank-eyed savages cowering before still blazing visor screens amid the rubble of palaces and iridescent buildings. They had landed on Petara, Karsten, Chandra: beautiful, ancient names, once famous. Sometimes, there had been disembodied subspace voices guiding them in, giving detailed instructions, allotting them landing space in immense spaceports where thousands of gigantic starships rotted. The police voices had been those of computers and still functioning robots, performing their last duties for a forgotten Empire. The vibrations from the landing scoutship caused buildings to totter and fall, burying the machinery beneath tons of smoking plastic and steel. The Empire had built well, but not for eternity. As the Confederation spread out, the old Empire died quietly.

And now Earth, the center of it all. After that: nothing.

'You look tired,' she said, leaning over him.

'I am. Forty hours without sleep usually makes me tired.' He sighed. 'Too much depends on this thing. I simply can't afford to let something happen while I'm snoring my head off. You haven't the faintest idea of how much the Confederation has sunk into this expedition. . . . You know, back to the old Empire center, glorious deeds, a whole treasure chest of a planet, everything waiting for us to pick up, and Thorein knows we need everything we can get. . . .' He relaxed, smiling at her. 'And now the whole bloody thing is starting to blow up in my face.'

It was damn easier to be a scout, he thought. *I wonder what it would be like, to do it again. To go out again, to the months in the ship, to the weeks on the planets. To be years ago again. And Cat again, for what it was worth.*

She said quietly, 'You've changed, Mon.'

'Everybody's changed. You. Me. Everybody. So what's strange about that? We have to grow up sometime, don't we?'

'You were different then,' she said. 'Softer. You're getting cynical.'

'Power,' he said, 'corrupts. You should see my soul, blackened by guilt. Sometimes I hate myself, but only sometimes. As for you . . .' He became silent.

'You want me back, don't you?' She smiled.

'I don't know. . . . No, I guess not. It's a good memory, on the whole. I like to keep my good memories good, when I can. Sometimes I want you back, but it's only good, clean lust, nothing else. The hairy animal.' He smiled vacantly.

She rose. 'You're practical,' she said.

'I'm a bastard, that's what you mean. Nothing wrong with that.' He leaned back in the chair again, watching her with amused interest. She was a bitch, he thought; a compassionate, beautiful, ever-understanding bitch. Calm, silent, and very, very beautiful. She always knew how to put her natural resources to the best possible use. Cat. A good name. The sleek, purring animal, graceful and lithe, sometimes even faithful. Independent as hell, and with a lot of sharp claws just in case.

He had walked out on her once: she hadn't liked that. Hurt her pride, probably, which would have been bad enough if she had been anyone else than sweet, patient Cat. She wasn't resentful, but she was stubborn. She always got what she wanted, in the end.

Legs tucked under her, because she knew he didn't care for legs anyway. If he had, they would have been displayed three inches from his eyes by now. She had her ways. He smiled.

'Who's the lucky one with the wandering key now?' he asked, rising. 'Anyone I know?'

'Do you care?'

'Not really. Just curious.'

She said, 'Dr. Gernstein. From sociology. I like him – he's amusing.' Frank, dispassionate.

'So. I've been wondering why the dreamy look.' He was standing by the disconnected visor screen, watching her reflection in the pearly gray glass. 'He's an ass.'

'That,' she said, 'is perhaps a matter of taste. I happen to like him.' She looked at him. 'Do you think that I throw myself at anyone who happens to come by?'

'A meeting of minds, then? Anyway, he's an ass. And probably wearing out both lock and key these days, if I know him.'

'It's a good lock,' Cat said, laughter in her eyes. 'It can take a lot of wear and tear.'

'But that key of his,' Monteyiller said, 'is in bad shape.'

'Are you offering me a new one?' She was laughing openly now.

'I think that lock of yours can take any key, any time. Besides, my own key is engaged elsewhere. Some other time.' He leaned over the maneuver console and pressed a button. The screen flickered to life, filled with the hovering ship's random search of the planet. He watched thoughtfully while the pictures succeeded each other, conscious of a warm glow in his face. And a pleasant tingle somewhere else.

The bitch, he thought amusedly. *The bloody impudent bitch. Start talking about anything at all, and within two sentences she's there.*

And, within two more sentences, he'd be there too.

He gazed intently at the screen, feeling her laughing eyes on his neck. Later, perhaps. He watched the glowing panorama, imprisoned behind the curved glass.

Cat smiled, but said nothing. That was one of her good qualities: she knew when to keep quiet.

16

A sun-burned desert flashed by on the screen, a steppe covered with slowly waving grass, a beach in the sunset, high dark trees in the background, and there on the beach a creature that gazed up at the sky. Monteyiller reached out and connected the camera for continuous surveying. The camera zoomed in on the creature, until it filled the whole screen.

At a distance and in the weak light, it had looked like a man on a horse, but in close-up it was different. It was a horse, but where the head should have been, the horse-body merged into the upper torso of a human being. It was a man, seemingly in middle-age, and he stood with his hands on his sides, gazing up at the sky. His long hair flowed in the wind, and his eyes gleamed with a vague intelligence. Monteyiller stood back, biting his lip.

'This,' he said, 'is what is commonly known as a centaur. See him?'

Cat jumped gracefully down from the table and came up to him. She eyed the creature with frank interest.

'A fabled beast from early Hellenic times,' she said lightly. 'A symbol of virility. A lecherous beast.'

She unconsciously passed her tongue over her lips.

'It was worshiped far into later Hellenic times, getting more and more lecherous with age. A nice specimen, isn't it?'

'There's never been any centaurs,' Monteyiller said. 'You have a filthy mind, that's all.'

'It must be a good year for nonexisting creatures,' Cat remarked. 'He's fat.'

'It *is* a centaur,' he admitted. 'Yet –'

'A biological experiment?'

'Why? And why a centaur?'

'The women might have liked him.' She smiled. 'But it is possible, though, isn't it? Fifty thousand years is a long time.'

Monteyiller didn't answer. He watched the screen, biting his lip. The centaur waved his tail a little, but didn't move.

'A flying horse,' he said tiredly, 'a giant bird, as big as one of our ships, two dragons – fire-breathing, no less – a giant gorilla . . . this is the sixth so-called fabled beast I've seen up

17

to now. So what's the matter with the bloody planet? Has it gone mad all of a sudden?'

He disconnected the screen with an angry gesture and walked away. Cat followed him out of the room, down the corridors. He kept his voice down for the sake of the people passing by on their way to their various duties. He was a popular captain, on the whole, but certain things are better not discussed too freely.

'So what am I supposed to do?' he asked. 'If I shoot the bloody things – which I would do, given half a chance – they'd probably turn out to be friendly and harmless, and I'd be the big trigger-happy fool. Or they might turn out to be nothing but fantasies, hallucinations, and I'd be a fool again, the big bully shooting away at shadows. H.Q. would crucify me. And if I don't shoot, you can bet they turn out to be vicious as hell, and H.Q. will ask me why didn't I vaporize the monsters right away. Naturally, I'd repeat what the computers said and H.Q. would tell me I had a brain myself, or I should have one! Damnit, what should I *do*?'

They went down the main corridor, and entered the ship's only canteen, which as usual was thronged with personnel. Most of the tables were occupied by tired-looking technical staff, who had been relieved by the night shift, sipping mildly alcoholic beverages. There was tension and impatience in the air. Something had to happen, Monteyiller thought, and fast. The fleet had been circling Earth for ten days now, doing nothing but monitoring the planet, and finally, today, sending down the scoutship. Probably everyone knew about the result by now.

They made their way between the crowded tables, exchanging greetings to right and left, and finally ended up at a vacant table in a corner. Monteyiller ordered two cups of pseudo-coffee from the dispenser and leaned over the table, pointedly avoiding the inquiring looks from the people near them.

'So what are you going to do?' Cat asked. 'Go down?'

'And risk the whole fleet?' He grimaced. 'We can't afford

that. This fleet was a great sacrifice for the Confederation. If we fail here, there won't be a new one. I'll play it very, very safe. . . . A new scoutship, perhaps, when Jocelyn and Martha are back, and then –' He looked thoughtfully at her. 'They're your business from now on, don't forget that. I want to know exactly what happened down there. You turn them inside-out if you have to; just make sure I get some answers.'

'If you're suggesting I use the probe on them, I won't.'

'I'm suggesting nothing. Do you think I want to destroy them? Put them on your couch and speak kindly to them, or use hypnosis or whatever you do – just remember that I need something fast.'

'You're asking for a lot,' Cat said quietly.

'There are people asking a lot of me too,' he said curtly. 'You have only me pestering you, but I have the whole bloody H.Q. breathing down my neck, demanding quick results because the Conservationists are breathing down *their* necks, howling for the termination of the whole project. They think this expedition is a waste of money, and they're partly right. So in the end it all comes down to me, and I'm passing the buck to you for the moment. Clear?' He smiled joylessly.

'Clear.'

He leaned back in the chair, feeling exhausted. Cat was regarding him with large, questioning eyes, with a frankness born out of two years of companionship. She knew, all right; she understood him. The tough captain of the fleet, the bright wonder-boy who always succeeded, and she looked right through him. But he needed her; she was the only one in whom he could confide.

It's too big for me, he thought. *Too bloody big, and there's no way out of it.*

He looked over her shoulder, at the visor screen placed by the far wall. Space filled the rectangle, unblinking stars, and silently floating dragonfly-ships. And down there under them, rolling like a rotting apple, stained with brown and blue, Earth. The continents could be vaguely discerned through specks and streaks of sluggishly floating clouds.

Fifty thousand years since the Exodus, and no one had visited it since. It had lived in the immense libraries of the new Empire, as a myth, a probability, a half forgotten memory without substance, without proof. Fifty thousand years was a long time; Empires had come and disappeared, dynasties had come and gone, immortal history was made and forgotten. The annals had become fables, facts had become superstitions. The Empire that had once deserted the mother planet for a new administrative center in the midst of its far-flung dominions had turned to dust millennia past, its successors hardly more than footnotes. Wars and disorder had taken their toll. Cultural and technological decline had made each planet its own kingdom. The long night closed in over the shattered remnants of the Empire, and Earth was a fable, a myth, the place of all dreams, the palace of light. There were religious cults worshiping it. And learned men argued that Earth never existed, that it was the ancient dream of Heaven.

And yet, here it was. The coordinates found in a ruined library somewhere. The Confederation of Planets, consisting of sixty-four formerly agricultural – and therefore unexploited – planets in an insignificant sector of the old Empire, took a chance and sent out an expedition. They could hardly afford it, but it was a risk worth taking. There might be things left on Earth, technical miracles spurned by the old Empire, unbelievable riches waiting to be taken. They came to scavenge in the rubbish left by the old Empire, eager, hopeful, and just a little bit afraid. The fourteen ships that circled around the planet were only the vanguard of another, far mightier armada of bureaucrats, soldiers and citizens which, after fifty thousand years of exile, prepared to return to the home planet. The ships circled patiently around the planet while the instruments searched after signs of human or mechanical activity. So far, there had been none, except for the monstrous beasts that the cameras picked up now and then. And the enormous structure, of course, the hallucination or whatever it might have been.

Monteyiller wondered what it was like down there as he

gazed at the scenes depicted in the visor screen: mountains, rivers, immense forests stretching away to the horizon. And the ever-present ruins. He shifted his eyes to Cat, who still regarded him.

'It's awesome, in a way,' he said, 'coming back to Earth . . . it frightens me. If the defense systems still worked and attacked us, it wouldn't scare me. That would be something tangible, something I could do something about. But this . . . I don't like it.'

'You don't understand it,' Cat said, shrugging. 'You never liked what you couldn't understand. *I* know that.'

He shot her an incisive glance. 'You mean yourself, don't you?'

'Well . . . in a way, yes.'

He looked up at the visor screen. 'You could be right,' he muttered. 'The planet is like a woman, just waiting for someone to come by. It's capricious and tricky, and you never know where you stand with her.'

'And yet you come to her,' Cat said. 'You aren't very wise, are you?'

'A purely accidental occurrence, for old times' sake, nothing else.' He rose abruptly. 'Come, let's go.'

She followed him out into the corridor. 'Where?' she asked.

'I've got work to do, that's all.' He looked up at a visor screen placed near the roof. Still nothing new. He sighed.

'In that case,' she said, 'I've got work to do, too.' She started down the corridor, then hesitated and turned. 'Call me if you need a key sometime, Mon. I just might have one for you.'

'The offer's still open, eh?' He grinned.

'It's never been closed.'

'Some other time, perhaps. Bye, Cat.' He turned around and strode down the corridor with quick, determined steps, toward the observations center. He smiled unconsciously, fingering the key-ring in his pocket. Cat was always so tactful. And he was practical; she had said so herself. He didn't need a new key. He had kept the old one all along.

21

4

On Earth: The white stallion descended softly from the sky and halted with a powerful thrust of the mighty wings in the air, a hundred feet above the ancient landing field. He hovered noiselessly above the ship, whose instruments cautiously observed him, decided that he didn't exist and unhurriedly proceeded to catalogue this new phenomenon into its files. The scoutships were highly intelligent, as robots go, but they had certain drawbacks – they didn't believe in fables. Pegasus was allowed to hang in the darkness unharmed, because, according to certain irrefutable laws of aerodynamics, this creature couldn't possibly behave that way, and the menacing disrupters which had trained themselves with deadly precision upon him, turned indifferently away. Untroubled, Pegasus gazed down at the man and woman who uncertainly walked away from the ship, and his eyes were big and shining and filled with a strange, infinite joy.

Far away in the brooding sky, Medea halted her coach in a shower of sparks, and the Valkyries gathered around her, wistfully looking down through the clouds. Behind the mountains, the Midgard serpent raised his colossal head over the snow-covered peaks and gazed with cold, piercing eyes at the two figures. The immense body, which clasped Earth like a girdle, trembled almost imperceptively. Mountains fell, rivers altered their courses, dust obscured the skies wherever the great body moved. Like an impenetrable shadow in the sky, the head hung, steadily looking down. Far behind all the others, the beetle Khepre stumbled over the clouds, joyously hurrying toward the old landing site, forgetting his age-old duties in his haste. The ship observed them all, noted their size and speed, decided that they didn't constitute any danger whatsoever, filed the information for further use and promptly forgot them. The robot in the maneuver chair was busy monitoring the progress of Martha and Jocelyn, and didn't pay any attention to the ship's doings.

The ship's disruptors swung uncertainly over the immense bulk of the Midgard serpent, but having decided that this monstrous creature apparently was yet another of those inexplicable phantoms, it lost interest in the creature and reverted to the less disquieting task of searching for more substantial intruders. It ignored sullenly the strange beings that gathered in the dark sky, whispering and muttering in the shadows, looking with strange and lonely eyes at the man and woman. All the fables of Man waited in the dusk, patiently as they had waited for fifty thousand years. The three old women who had prophesied Man's return, sat beneath the tree Yggdrasil, under a dark and brooding sky, spinning threads for their terrible web, while a dark man in a billowing cloak silently looked on. A certain dragon gnawed on the tree's roots; his name was Nidhögg. And on the crest of a white-capped mountain, the Earth-goddess Demeter Chamyne waited with her court of bald men, so eminently suited for her purposes. She threw back her lustrous hair with a toss of her head and looked up at the sky, where Khepre happily stumbled on toward the landing field, and laughed.

Beyond the ruins: Jocelyn.

In the pale light of the moon, he walked down a steep slope, Martha at his heels, gun like a relic in his hand. There were soughing trees at both sides, ghostly pale in the moonlight; brittle plaster crumbled under his feet. His eyes darted from side to side, searching the dusk for signs of attack, and finding nothing but brooding shadows. When he looked up at the sky, the stars were feeble and few, and a large portion of the sky was devoid of stars, as if some incredible huge object was blotting them out. Strange noises could be heard in the distance, like the rustling of dry leaves, tittering and whispering creatures in the dark, silently creeping nearer. He shrugged, and continued.

He had convinced himself that it was a hallucination, after all. It made him feel better, but it also started him wondering. He walked down the slope, pupils widened, wondering what he saw, wondering what Martha saw. Neither of them spoke about it.

The slope narrowed into a depression: cliffs appeared, and precipitous clefts. The landscape was gashed, mutilated, torn. In the cliffs, sedimental strata marched in hundreds of parallel ribbons: blue, gray, yellow, brown, red. And an abundance of fossils: Liparoceras, Cubitostrea, Trilobites. The strata started at Proterozoic time, at the foot of the cliffs, and went up to Quaternary and beyond. Petrified Crinoids and Cephalopods littered the ground at their feet; above them, the ruins of Man brooded under the sky, where the spaceships silently spread their iridescent wings. Once, a mighty river had flowed here.

It narrowed more: into a gorge, a chasm enclosed by bluff cliffs, towering darkly over them. Still they walked down the narrowing path, secure in the knowledge of the man-robot and the sentient dragonfly-ship, waiting among the ruins behind them. Dark moss clung to the cliffs, and phosphoric growths. There was the sound of whisperings and small clawed feet, scraping against weathered stone. They turned around a jagged bend of the gorge, and saw the creature, crouched on a beetling cliff above them, watching them with large, unaverted eyes.

The Sphinx: It was part woman, part beast. She had feathered wings, rising like a crown over her back; claws; powerful tail; and the thin, graceful brows of a beautiful woman's eyes. She had a lithe feline body, the ruffled wings of a giant bird, the slender neck of a woman, proudly rising out of feathers and sleek, golden feline hair. She looked at them, and spoke with a voice that was musical and clear.

'You come through my pass. Very well, then: you must answer my riddle, then you may pass. If not . . .' Claws appeared on her paws, black and deadly.

Jocelyn is still secure (*the man-robot; the sentient ship; power*). 'What's this?' he asked.

'The Theban Sphinx,' she said, smiling beautifully. 'The ·Throttler, the Choker, the Tight-binder, the Guardian of the Pass, the Demon of Death. I was sent here by Hera; I give riddles; I guard the pass. Only one has solved my riddle, a man with black eyes and swollen feet who limped by on his way to a mother unknown. Now I will give you the riddle.' She smiled again.

'It's like a talking parrot,' Jocelyn said, 'but horrible.' He peered at the Sphinx, who crouched in the pearly light of the moon. 'A machine?'

Martha had retreated back into the shadows. 'Let's go back.'

'I am swift as Death,' the Sphinx said, looking at her. 'You will never get away unless you solve my riddle.'

'A joke,' Jocelyn said contemptuously. (*The man-robot, the ship, gun in hand, cool metal and slumbering fire: a sense of power.*) 'Perhaps it can do tricks.' He grinned at the Sphinx. 'Can you?'

'I don't like this,' Martha said. 'Let's go back.'

'It's only a robot or something! Are you scared?'

'Yes.' Strained.

The Sphinx said, 'Are you ready for the riddle?'

'Sure. Shoot.'

'Now,' she said, 'listen.'

> 'A thing there is whose voice is one,
> Whose feet are two and four and three.
> So mutable a thing is none
> That moves in earth or sky or sea.
> When on most feet this thing doth go
> Its strength is weakest and its pace most slow.'

There was silence. After a while, the Sphinx smiled. Claws appeared. Muscles strained for the leap; the wings folded out.

Lazily, the Sphinx rose on her legs, shifting her eyes from one to the other.

'The riddle,' she said, 'is nought for you to solve; and having failed, as all flesh must fail, I will devour you.'

The wings spread out.

'For heaven's sake!' Martha cried. 'Run!'

The Sphinx leaped.

In the ship, the robot gazed at the visor screen. There were moving forms, pale in the bleak white lights; the flashing of a gun momentarily froze the picture into a blinding white caricature of life. The man was locked in the embrace of the Sphinx; the woman was crouching on the ground, widened eyes gleaming and white. Fire streamed from her hand, and dissipated. The Sphinx was unharmed.

The robot was quiet and methodical. He swiveled the chair around, hands reaching for the maneuver console. In the flickering light from the screen, he moved like a smoothly animated puppet among the shadows and the blinking red and blue lights. He touched buttons, levers, dials. There was the hum of awakening machinery, swelling and rising, climbing up the scale and disappearing, the sound of mechanisms being retracted into the hull and others taking their places. Gleaming black barrels swung into position, trajectories were calculated. The maneuver console dazzled with light.

The screen scanned the landing site, surrounded by brooding ruins, silent and quiet. The robot gave the order for ascent. The ship lifted obediently, but stopped again.

Dark forms appeared, looming around the ship, perceived only by the ship. The visor screen still showed the open plain, ringed by ruins, but the ship registered walls of stone, rapidly rising all around. Steep cliffs grew out of the ground, rising and closing in above. They formed a cavern, dripping with moisture and dark. Glittering with light, stalagmites and stalactites appeared, forming pillars, and arches, draperies. They enclosed the ship in a cage of magnificent crystalline bars, glittering with the light of emeralds, tourmalines, and chrysolites. The ship's mass detectors registered billions of tons of stone enclosing the cave. It hesitated, hovering beneath the impenetrable roof, then descended to the ground again, refusing to move.

The robot saw nothing of this: only the open plain, the sky. He touched the buttons, gave orders, but the ship stayed put. Finally, he leaped out of the chair, grabbed weapons and ran out through the airlock. The ship watched him run away between pillars of frozen fire, only to disappear in unyielding rock. It was puzzled, but the instruments showed the cave to be there. It filed the information and forgot about it.

The robot raced down the slope, toward the gorge where the black mass of Jocelyn and the Sphinx was tumbling on the ground. Martha lay huddled behind a boulder nearby, white-faced. The robot dropped the weapon and threw himself at the Sphinx, metallic hands tearing at her flesh. The Sphinx flung away Jocelyn, who hit the rocks with a sickening thud and lay still, and then turned against the robot. The robot was quick and intelligent and methodical; the Sphinx was old, old, and cunning. She circled around him, smiling.

'My riddle applies not to you,' she said, 'and Hera never thought your likeness would come. I cannot devour you; but where life is, life must be taken, and there is life in you, the flickering light of life. So may it be.' She lunged forward. The robot moved away, but not quite fast enough. There was the sound of tearing metal, a crunch, a heavy fall. The Sphinx rose slowly and returned to Jocelyn. Martha, momentarily forgotten, also rose, her eyes staring blindly at the creature. Then she turned around and ran.

The ship was no longer alone. A yellow-haired girl in a blue dress came out of the cave-wall and entered the ship. She sat in the maneuver chair, looking at the whirling kaleidoscopic patterns of the visor screen and kicked her feet in delight. The ship gave no signs of noticing her. There were buttons and dials in the armrest of the chair, multicolored and blazing with light. Strange things occurred when she pushed them, and her mischievous eyes glittered with unrestrained joy.

5

Monteyiller raced down the main corridor of the flagship, his eyes still clouded with sleep. His boots made a hollow sound on the steel floor, echoed by the running steps of the young and nervous lieutenant who had awakened him.

He had gone to sleep, at last; that, he thought grimly, was the mistake. Something was bound to turn up. He swore under his breath, as he swung into the command room.

'Okay!' he shouted over the din in the room. 'I'm here! Now quiet down, so I can see what's up!' He elbowed his way through the small room crowded with excited personnel and thankfully sank down in a chair vacated by a red-eyed technician. He yawned and rubbed his eyes, feeling terrible.

'Okay,' he said, somewhat calmer, 'somebody please tell me what's happening.' In an undertone, he added, 'I'm probably going to be crucified for this anyway, so I might as well know what it's about.'

'It's the scoutship,' somebody said. 'You know, Martha and Jocelyn –'

'So I gathered. What's happened?'

'They've been attacked.'

'*What?*' He straightened up, the sleepiness disappearing in an instant. 'How?'

Edy Burr appeared between him and the control console. 'The computers,' he said uncertainly, 'don't give any –'

'Damn the computers! What happened?'

'The instruments don't agree as to what's happened, that's all,' interjected a voice which he recognized as belonging to the watch-officer, a small man with a permanently perplexed look and a brooding black moustache. 'The video link has one version, the data processing unit of the scoutship has another.' He swallowed. 'It's very disturbing, sir.'

'Everything is disturbing in this place,' Monteyiller muttered. 'Where are Martha and Jocelyn now?'

There was a brief pause. Then Edy coughed. 'We believe they were . . . killed,' he said quietly.

'You're mad!' Monteyiller rose halfway out of his chair. 'They can't be! The ship would have prevented it!'

'The ship,' Edy said, 'says it was in a stalactite cave, with miles of rock surrounding it in all directions.'

'That's a real good one,' Monteyiller said curtly. 'What about the robot? Was he in some stalactite cave, too?'

'He tried to intervene,' Edy said. He hesitated. 'We believe he was destroyed in the process. I'm sorry, Mon, but that's how it is.'

'That's true?' he asked quietly. 'Just like that?'

'Yes. I'm sorry.'

Somebody thrust a cup of pseudo-coffee in Monteyiller's hands. He sipped it slowly, looking over the brim at the group that surrounded him.

'You there,' he said, looking at the watch-officer. 'What happened, exactly?'

'They decided to go on with the search,' the watch-officer said. 'We spoke a lot about it, first, but then they became convinced that it had been some sort of hallucination after all –'

'I see you didn't exactly discourage them,' Monteyiller commented dryly. 'Okay, go on.'

'They came down in a gorge just outside the landing site, and there was a creature –' He hesitated. 'There's a recording from the ship. It's better if you look at that.'

Monteyiller snapped, 'Turn it on.'

He leaned forward in the chair as the screen before him lighted up with the picture of the ghostly, moonlit gorge and the creature, crouched on the protruding cliff over Martha's and Jocelyn's heads. He stiffened.

'Thorein!' he gasped. 'A Sphinx!'

'You know what that is?' The watch-officer was clearly bewildered.

'Shut up!' He gazed intently at the screen, as the drama was played over again, thoughts whirling around in his head. It was unbelievable, impossible – yet here it was, complete in the last little detail. Even the riddle was there. He looked silently at the swiftly moving shadows, a sick feeling spreading inside him.

The recording ended, and Monteyiller looked up at the silent group that surrounded him. 'Anybody recognize it?' he asked. He looked for Cat, but couldn't find her in the room. Instead, his gaze fell on Dr. Gernstein, who stood tall and aloof by the atrogator sphere, his eyes fixed on the visor screen. 'You, Dr. Gernstein, don't you recognize it?' He suddenly became aware of the hysterical note in his voice, and sank back, cursing himself.

'What do you mean?' Dr. Gernstein asked. 'Recognize? Is this some kind of joke . . . ?'

Monteyiller drew deeply for breath. His hands flexed and unflexed on the armrests of the chair. 'I'm sorry,' he muttered. 'It was nothing. I was . . . wrought up, I guess. . . . Martha got away. What became of her?'

'We don't know,' Edy said.

'I see.' Monteyiller frowned. 'And Jocelyn just might be living. I didn't see the . . . creature actually kill him.'

'But you saw what happened!' Edy exclaimed. 'You can't believe that he came through *that*!'

'I see what I see!' Monteyiller snapped. 'And I surely didn't see anything worse than a rough tumble. Jocelyn is a tough man; he can take care of anything, in one way or another. And as for that robot, it wasn't made for fighting anyway.' He bit his lip thoughtfully. 'What about that ship? Let's see the visual recordings from the so-called cave.'

The screen showed the desolate plain, unmoving beneath the moon. Cliffs appeared, walls closed in over the ship, pillars grew, glittering with crystal light. The dials registered uncountable tons of unyielding rock in all directions.

Monteyiller sighed.

'So that's the famous cave,' he said. 'What a performance!' He looked up. 'You had contact with the ship all the time, you say?'

'Yes.'

'Then why didn't the cave shield the transmission? There are billions of tons of rock there, and the transmitters are good, sure, but not *that* good. There isn't a signal in the whole universe that could have penetrated that mass! So how could you receive this?'

There was silence. Finally, Edy said, 'But the instruments –'

'The instruments! That blasted ship just conked out for good, that's all. First that cathedral, and now this. I don't care if every instrument bears it out, it's just downright impossible that there could have been any cave there. And if it wasn't any cave . . .' He left the sentence unfinished.

'Martha and Jocelyn saw the cathedral too,' Edy said stiffly.

'Yeah. That's what's bothering me.' Monteyiller rose from the chair and walked toward the door. 'Something funny is going on down there, I grant you that – but I won't take the ship's word for it.' He cast a glance up at the wall clock. 'I'm going down myself. Prepare for launching of another scout-ship in . . . fifteen minutes. And keep contact with the ship down there. That's all.' He turned abruptly around and left the room.

He found Cat in one of the briefing rooms, looking through a library spool with ancient folklore of Earth. A three-dimensional picture of a centaur hung in the air before her. Monteyiller sank down on a chair beside her.

'Doing research on our virile friend down there?'

'A little.' She switched off the projector and turned to him. 'Has something come up?'

'That's the very least you could say.' He briefly related the incident, describing the creature in detail. 'It was straight out

31

of one of those psychological plays you showed me once. . . .' He searched for it. 'Orestes something.'

'King Oedipus.' She nodded slowly. 'An ancient play by Sophocles. And the riddle, too. . . .' She looked up at him. 'You're sure there isn't somebody pulling your leg? It's too much of a coincidence.'

'Nobody here knows a single line from any King Oedipus, or from any other play for that matter. Besides, this is too grave; nobody would joke about that.'

'A robot actor or something?'

'Could be. But it should be a hell of a robot to work like that after fifty thousand years.' He leaned toward her. 'Look, I don't like this, it's . . . uncanny. All those fantastic creatures running around everywhere, centaurs, dragons, this Sphinx . . . and the ship is starting to get hallucinations, too. The machines are about the only thing in the world that one can trust – they don't lie – and now they're starting to behave strangely too. I –' He paused, hesitated. 'We're going down,' he said abruptly.

'The whole ship? I thought you didn't dare risk it.'

'A scoutship. Room for three, the robot included.' He looked thoughtfully at her. 'We'll need a psychologist, preferably one with extensive knowledge of the old folklore of Earth.'

'I get the hint.' She smiled.

He rose. 'We made a good pair once. It could work out again.'

'The good old team. . . .' She turned around. 'It's a deal, Mon, I'll go.'

The sound of his hurried steps disappeared in the echoing corridor, and as Cat briskly started to collect the library spools, her smile faded and her mouth hardened.

6

On Earth: the landscape stabilized into new forms. In the crumbling spaceport, the scoutship still hovered unmovingly, imprisoned by forces perceived only by itself. The gorge was no more; where it had been a dark forest began, stretching away toward the horizon. And far away in the forest: Martha.

Martha walked down an ancient stone-paved road, the shadow crawling grotesquely after her. The dim forest spread silently out around her, in the first jagged light of dawn. The rising sun gleamed in her black hair and her large, frightened eyes. There were cedars, birches, and the gnarled trunks of old, old oaks around her; and behind her, soft green light filtered down through the dense crowns of beeches. There were echoes of birds and distant winds, the rustling of leaves, the sound of hidden streams: orchestras played in the still, timeless sea of the sleeping forest.

She stumbled on, haunted by the memory of the Sphinx and the bloodied piece of flesh that had been someone she knew. The scene had played over and over again behind her closed eyelids as she had run through the silent forest, crying out at the impenetrable night, stumbling, falling, crawling, recoiling in horror at the slightest sound and weeping with the unreasonable fear of the unknown. There had been beings in the night, silently running beside her, slitted eyes gleaming with light of their own and disappearing when she lunged after them. The night had been endless, filled with the sounds of her own labored breathing and formless shadows creeping nearer and disappearing again. And when the dawn came at last, they melted away in the shadows of the brooding trees, so swiftly and noiselessly that she wondered if they ever had existed.

Martha walked on, only halfway conscious of the forest surrounding her. The forest was a dream, the ship was a dream, only the memory of Jocelyn dying was real. Behind her frozen face, she was crying.

Suddenly she heard voices behind a small grove by the road. Her hand darted automatically down to the useless gun that hung at her thigh, its fire spent on an invincible beast half a night and an eternity ago; then she cautiously crept up to the grove. There were laughing voices of men and women, speaking in an oddly archaic but still recognizable tongue. The sweet voices seemed to pose no danger. She parted the branches and looked down on a small sunlit-glade, filled with strange beings. There were girls in bright dresses, iridescent gossamer wings spreading from their backs, dwarfs, men and women dressed in flowing robes, and there – Martha's eyes widened – a small, fat man with an ass's head, sitting on the ground, while a strangely beautiful woman in a dress of a thousand colors bent over him, caressing the animal head and talking, her voice soft and low.

As Martha gazed down at the strange scene in the glade, there was a slight sound behind her, and something touched her arm. She whirled around.

The little yellow-haired girl in the blue dress looked up at her, hands behind her back, wearing a look of blank inquiry.

'A midsummer night's dream,' she said. 'Do you like it?' She hesitated shyly. 'I mean, the fairies? It is nice, isn't it?'

Martha was silent. The girl took a step toward her and smiled suddenly. 'I thought that perhaps you would like it,' she said.

Martha asked slowly, 'Who are you?'

'Alice.' The smiling eyes held Martha's, the mischievous childish eyes, with laughter hidden behind the blue irises. 'I live here.'

'Here?'

'Well, not exactly here, but not far away. . . . You didn't seem happy, but you liked the fairies, didn't you?'

Martha found herself smiling in response. 'Perhaps.'

34

'What do you want?' the girl asked.

Martha looked down at Alice, painful joyous laughter in her throat. It was so amusing, so incredibly, impossibly amusing. Did she want anything? What was there to want? Didn't she have everything anyone could wish for? There was beauty around her, peace, love. Only –

'Jocelyn,' she said. 'I want Jocelyn.' She still smiled, her face frozen in a painful grimace of forced joy. 'But he is dead,' she said.

A corner of her mind screamed at her: *Why am I doing this? What is happening to me? Why am I saying this?*

Aloud, she repeated, 'But he is dead,'

The girl stared at her. 'Oh,' she said slowly.

Martha turned back to the grove. She felt dazed, drunken. A warm feeling of happiness and well-being slowly spread through her body, drowning out the small, insistent voice that kept asking *Why, why, why.* She smiled drowsily and looked down into the glade. It was deserted.

She giggled.

Something moved in the dusk beyond the glade. A tall, shadowed man came into view, his face hidden in the dark. He called softly out to her.

'Martha?'

Her vision blurred as she ran through the grass. 'Jocelyn!' she cried. 'Jocelyn!' She cried and laughed at the same time.

Behind her, Alice stood, gazing at the grove. Wind rustled and a rabbit jumped up at her, begging for attention. She bent down and fondled it absently. The rabbit whined happily.

Martha reached the glade, embracing, embraced. The glade was filled with light, yet the man's face was still shadowed. He looked like Jocelyn, but then he didn't. It was a Jocelyn seen through Martha's eyes, a strange, idealized, stylized Jocelyn. He had a gash over his right eye. His clothes were torn. His voice was almost that of Jocelyn. Almost, but not quite. It was the voice of a Jocelyn only Martha knew.

'Are you happy?' the warm, disembodied voice asked. 'Really?'

35

She smiled and closed her eyes.

On the other side of the grove, Alice scooped up the rabbit in her arms and ran away into the dim forest, leaving the small, sunlit glade where Martha stood, transfixed by someone who could have been Jocelyn.

7

Monteyiller's ship fell down from the sky engulfed in a sphere of glowing, iridescent light, followed by the drawn-out roar of a continuous sonic boom. Compressed air hit the ruins with the force of a thousand sledgehammers, toppling them down in clouds of dust.

He handled the ship like a bucking horse, hard, unyielding, ruthlessly. The ship's brain was disconnected from the landing circuits; his agile fingers danced over the flashing buttons of the maneuver console with dizzying speed, steering, correcting, calculating. His gaze was fixed on the visor screen where the landscape rushed by, made into an indistinct haze by the speed. His eyes glittered, his lips drawn back in an almost painful grimace. Cat, in the chair beside him, closed her eyes and leaned back.

Just like old times again, the mad dash down, the destruction, the happiness in his face. She had seen that expression many times before, too many times before, and she hated it. She let out her breath slowly, pictures flashing by behind her eyelids. They had been together like that for two years, rambling through the galaxy, seeking new pastures for the Confederation, new riches to be exploited, new planets for an ever-growing population. The old colonies were rediscovered as scoutships descended, engulfed in spheres of iridescent light roaring above the ancient cities and the ruins of former splendor, with destruction in their wake, the air thundering with sonic booms. The New Empire rising: the sound of progress. They had been one of the best scout teams at the time: quick, reliable and, above all, surviving. The combination had proven itself: calm, compassionate, cunning Cat, the psychologist, the scholar, the beautiful; and Monteyiller, the fierce tornado of a man, the autocrat, the wonder-boy with the hard eyes and the set mouth and the desperate mind. It had been a good time, on the whole, but when they were promoted in the ranks, they left the scouting and each other without regrets. Two years had been enough and more than enough; they knew each other too well, after spending months at a stretch alone in the scoutship and on desolate, lifeless planets, waiting to be picked up by the returning fleet. Love-making kept them together at times, but that was plain and simple lust, without love, the defense against boredom, loneliness and human needs. Silently, they had hated each other.

Her mouth set as the ship raged over the mountains, the desolate plains, the slumbering forests, the dead cities that turned into flying dust behind them. Morning was coming; the clouds were oceans of fire, billowing up over the sky, reflecting in running waters and fragments of broken glass. There would be birds singing down there, and dark shapes awakening in the fermenting jungles. And somewhere, a man and a woman, and something which had been neither. The remnants of the scout team: alone, frightened, dying. The riddle of the Sphinx: the ages of Man. The closing circle: the absolute, inevitable end. She shuddered as the ship bore down, howling like a dark demon, toward the landing site.

The ruins flowed in the morning light and shimmered like mist, slowly stabilizing into new and unknown shapes, stirring with the life of the ancient fables of Man.

The scarred metal of the landing field heaved and became a landscape of low, rolling hills covered with succulent green grass. The mist descended to the ground and formed fairy-rings, waving over the grass. Peacocks solemnly treaded the grass, and there were starlings, robins and swans, and rabbits and kittens, white with pink noses. The air was filled with the scents of bygone summers, the sounds of worlds lost.

And there was the house, which was as no other house, standing on a low grass-covered hill. Its chimneys were shaped like a hare's ears and the roof was thatched with fur;

and under a tree in front of the house there was a table set out with teapots and cups and plates for the benefit of a hare dressed in a blue suit, and a dormouse and a small man with a large black hat. They were all crowded together at one corner of the table, and no one took any notice of the scoutship as it came thundering down in a wide flaming curve from the sky, burning the grass to cinders, sending the age-old trees spinning in the air: the burning monuments of Man returning.

The ship came to a stop a hundred yards from the curious house, hovering silently two feet over the ground. Monteyiller leaned forward in the chair, studying the visor screen.

'Look at that hallucination!' He scowled. 'It's practically real. No wonder Martha and Jocelyn fell for it.'

'If the hallucinations were so real that the ship couldn't light from the ground,' Cat said, 'they'd be real enough for us too.'

'What's eating you? You think it is *real*?'

'It might be.'

'You're out of your mind. Did you ever see creatures like that?' He grinned at her. 'Even if they turn out to be real, that's all the better. I can handle anything that's real, be it a bloody hare in a business suit or what-have-you.' He reached out and flipped a switch, activating the ship's brain. 'I want a sample taken of the ground under the ship,' he said. 'Make an analysis of it and report. No thorough examination, just tell me if it's metal or stone or soil or whatever.' He turned to Cat. 'That'll show you.'

There was silence while the ship scooped up a sample of the ground and made a brief analysis of it, then:

'A very simple analysis,' the ship said, 'shows the ground to be of ordinary Earth soil, very fertile, with numerous microorganisms. The soil is covered with vegetable growth of the species Graminae, which is commonly known as –'

'It's enough,' Cat interrupted. She looked at him. 'It means grass.'

'Grass?'

'Yes, grass. What did you expect it to be?'

Monteyiller swiveled the chair around and got up, swearing. 'This is beautiful!' he said. 'The damn ship's conked out too! Look here – this place was a landing field ten minutes ago. I saw it with my own eyes, so how in hell can it be grass now?'

'But it is.' She smiled.

'It can't be. You're going to see for yourself. Let's get out of here.'

The airlock opened. Outside, the green landscape stretched on to the horizon, unbroken except for magnificent ancient trees and the curious house. Monteyiller made a vile grimace at it.

'Grass!' he said contemptuously.

It was grass. Monteyiller rose from his crouching position outside the ship, a curious expression on his face.

'Well, I'll be damned,' he muttered. He looked at Cat. 'Seems I miscalculated in the ship's navigation. This isn't the landing field.' He turned to the robot. 'Where are we?'

The robot said, 'At the place where the first ship landed. You navigated correctly.'

'I did, eh? So where is the other ship, then?'

The robot pointed. 'According to the calculations, there.'

'You're mad. That's a house. So you see a ship there, eh?'

'I see a house,' the robot said unconcernedly. 'However, according to the calculations, the ship should be there.'

Monteyiller looked at the house. It was unnatural, all right, with the animals sitting at the table, right out of some fairy tale for very small children. And the pastoral scenery where the ruins of the spaceport should have been.

Illusions.

Earth gone mad; dreams turned sour; insecurity; old fear awakening.

Somebody, he thought, *is playing a joke on me.*

He corrected himself: *Us.*

The bastard.

He started off toward the odd house.

The three at the table eyed him with obvious disapproval. 'No room! No room!' they cried out when they saw him approaching. He didn't pay any attention to them, but sat down in a large armchair at one end of the table, only slightly surprised at finding it substantial and hard to the touch. He leaned forward, putting his elbows on the table, gazing at them. 'There *is* room,' he said.

'Have some wine,' the hare said in an encouraging tone.

Monteyiller looked over the table. There was nothing on it but tea. 'I don't see any wine,' he said.

'There isn't any,' said the hare.

'So why invite me to wine when there isn't any?' Monteyiller asked, momentarily confused.

'So why invite yourself to sit down when you aren't invited?' said the hare. 'You and your funny friends.'

Monteyiller's eyebrows shot up. 'They don't sit,' he said.

'They would only *dare*!' said the hare agitatedly.

'Your hair wants cutting,' said the small man with the big hat. He had been looking at Monteyiller for some time with great curiosity, and this was his first speech.

'He is an imagined creature,' the hare said knowingly. 'They *always* look like that.'

'Unkempt, yes.'

'Very unkempt.'

'And one of his friends has a watch ticking inside his chest. I don't think it is very civil, to come uninvited to tea with a watch ticking inside one's chest.'

'It's the same with all imagined creatures; they have no manners at all,' said the hare, looking disapprovingly at the robot.

'The dormouse is sleeping again,' said the man with the hat, and he poured a little hot tea on its nose.

The dormouse shook its head impatiently, and said, without opening its eyes, 'Of course, of course; just what I was going to remark myself.'

'Why is a raven like a writing desk?' the man with the hat asked, looking sharply at Monteyiller.

41

'It was the *best* butter,' the hare muttered uneasily.

'Once upon a time there were three little sisters,' the dormouse began in a great hurry, 'and their names were –'

'Some tea, perhaps?' the man with the hat asked politely.

'. . . perhaps some crumbs got into the watch as well,' the hare said meekly.

'. . . ticking inside his *chest*!'

'What day is it? My watch has stopped again.'

'. . . shouldn't have put it in with the bread knife . . .'

They began to speak agitatedly to each other, forgetting the visitors in their argumenting for and against. Monteyiller looked from one to another, wondering if he was sane. Finally, as the discussion went on and no one took any interest in him, he rose from the chair and walked back to Cat and the robot, who had stopped some way from the table, looking silently at the strange scene.

'Don't ask me,' he said wearily, 'because I haven't the foggiest idea.'

Cat said, 'Didn't you recognize it?'

Monteyiller stared at her. 'Me? Why?'

'It's the Mad Tea Party, from an ancient story. I read it once: *Alice in Wonderland*.'

'It's mad, all right,' Monteyiller muttered. 'So what?'

She looked past him, pursing her lips. 'It could be robots.'

'Sure, robots.' He didn't sound convinced.

She walked by him, up to the table where the three beings steadfastly refused to take any notice of her. They were dissecting a large pocket watch, the innards of which was partially filled with rich golden butter, lavishly sprinkled with breadcrumbs.

'I told you butter wouldn't suit the works!' said the man with the hat, looking angrily at the hare.

'It was the *best* butter,' the hare replied meekly.

'They're like the robots in the amusement parks,' Cat said doubtfully, looking at them. She turned to Monteyiller. 'We might have landed right in the middle of some kind of amusement park; that would account for all this.'

'A damn queer sense of humor they must have had,' Monteyiller muttered, 'with that bloody Sphinx tearing people to pieces.'

'They've been here for fifty thousand years,' Cat said. 'Machines break down sooner or later.'

'You're a genius,' Monteyiller said sarcastically. He walked past her, toward the house. 'Don't forget to tell me if you get any more bright ideas, will you? And start moving, there's people here somewhere, needing help. Let's go.'

Cat came after him. 'You think the ship is there?' she asked incredulously.

'How should I know? It just might be, that's all.'

She sighed, but didn't say anything.

They entered the house. There was magnificent disorder: shoes placed on the hat-racks, tables turned upside-down and teacups balancing on the legs, bird cages with strange animals which definitely were not birds. The place was quiet and peaceful, and so absurd that Cat couldn't help smiling.

'Look, Mon,' she began, 'isn't it –'

She was cut off by the door behind them slamming shut in the face of the approaching robot. She whirled around, and gasped.

The air began to shimmer around them, mist poured out from the walls, momentarily obscuring them from view. There was the feeling of space opening all around, and a damp chill coming from all directions. The sounds from the green landscape were replaced by an ominous silence, punctuated by a steady dropping in the distance. Monteyiller was groping forward in the whirling mist, swearing profusely and calling out her name; his boots rang out on hard unyielding stone.

Suddenly, the mist cleared and disappeared. They were standing in an immense stalactite cave, softly lit by some unknown source, scintillating pillars rising up toward the dark roof somewhere high, high above. Cat staggered backward and came upon the stone wall. It was hard and moist to the

43

touch. Monteyiller stood, crouched, gun in his hand, staring at an object in the center of the cave.

There, encircled by iridescent pillars, sparkling with the light of rubies and emeralds and chrysolites, a black scoutship hovered unmovingly two feet over the ground. Its weapons were retracted into the hull, the airlock was closed. It just hung there, Jocelyn's and Martha's invincible, magnificent, trapped ship.

8

Monteyiller leaned back in the maneuver chair, a pained expression on his face. He banged his fist in the armrest, spread out the fingers and stared at them as if seeking consolation in the throbbing pain.

'So it's the real ship, all right,' he said slowly, 'and untouched, too. But as to that bloody cave . . .' He looked up at the curved screen facing him. It showed the interior of the enormous cave, bathed in the strange pale light that seemed to come from all directions; but the picture wavered and rippled as if it weren't quite sure that the cave really was there. Occasionally, a green, rolling landscape could be seen through the rock walls, brief snatches of trees and grass that came and went, exploded into view and reluctantly faded away. Without the aid of the visor screen, the rock was as impenetrable as before, and the ship's brain stubbornly maintained that the cavern was *there*, completely and irrevocably. Whatever it was that had created the illusion, it had done its job well. Only the cameras weren't completely fooled.

'This is it,' he said tightly, staring at the flickering screen. 'Trapped in a hallucination, and no way out.' He swiveled the chair around until he faced Cat, in the other maneuver chair. 'Any ideas?'

She said, 'We could blast our way out. There are disrupters in the ship, and –'

'And get the whole damn roof down on our heads? No thanks!' He raised his hand when she opened her mouth to protest. 'Sure, I know it's only a hallucination, but if we started to blast away with the disrupters, you can bet your sweet neck the roof would come down anyway, hallucination or not. I won't take any risks.' He swung back toward the screen, his mouth hardening into a thin bloodless line.

Cat said, 'Do you have any better ideas?'

He hesitated. 'Well . . . perhaps not. But I'm not going to take this lying down. Look, you've been around as much as I have, and you know what devilish tricks alien life can play on you. This smells so fishy it chokes me!'

Cat rose from her chair and went over to the airlock. She leaned against the curved wall and looked out. 'But this isn't alien,' she said over her shoulder. 'This is Earth.'

'Sure.' He watched her reflection on the screen, superimposed on the wavering picture of the cavern. 'Sure. Earth. But Earth hasn't been visited for fifty thousand years, and that's a mighty long time. Do you think everyone that stayed behind dropped dead when the Empire left? I'd say no. Anything could have happened since then.' He frowned. 'There are a lot of things that can make humans or aliens exert themselves, but in the end it all comes down to the old bellyful, nothing else. They might be cannibals, for all I know, and this might be the way to their bloody kitchen.'

Cat's eyebrows shot up. 'Do you really believe in that?'

'I believe in nothing. I'm just trying to get along with this whole madness.'

He rose from the chair, disconnecting the screen with a flick of his hand. The picture shrank to a brilliant dot of light and disappeared. 'We're getting out,' he said.

She turned slowly around toward him. 'How?'

'What do you think?' He was rummaging through a small closet set in the wall, throwing things out on the floor at his feet. He straightened up with two ultrawave transceivers in his hands. He threw one of them to her; she caught it deftly and hung it over her shoulder. 'Hallucination or not, there's only one way out of this place – the good, old, unscientific method.'

He checked his transceiver as he talked. Then he walked past her through the airlock and jumped down on the outside. He pointed to the far end of the immense cavern. Far away, new caverns opened up, burning with petrified light.

'Walking!'

They left the trapped scoutship behind. Frozen waterfalls sprang into view, bridges leading from nowhere to nowhere, sculptured from stone and dripping water for millennia – or seconds of inexplicable creation. Monteyiller didn't want to guess; and deep inside, he knew with chilling conviction that he was afraid of finding the answers.

They entered a petrified forest where mighty trees rose up toward the distant roof, their roots embraced by bushes and undergrowth of cold gleaming stone, stout branches reaching out in the air, still bearing petrified leaves, the bushes still bearing flowers in glowing crystalline colors, the grass frozen, bowing for a wind that died out a million years ago. A narrow trail wound between the imposing trees, paralleled by a brook with clear, glittering water. It rushed down in miniature waterfalls, sending sprays of cool water up in the air, washing the smooth stones along its banks to a silver luster. No other sound was heard except that of the water, echoing between trees and bushes and grass of unmoving, beautiful stone. They walked carefully down the meandering trail. The ground was hard and brittle and crunched under their feet. The forest was still and silent as death.

'It's impressive as hell,' Monteyiller said, pausing to mop his perspiring forehead. 'Nothing like this back home.'

'It's beautiful,' Cat agreed.

'It gives me the jitters,' Monteyiller said. 'I hate it.'

'Well, it's certainly a – *Mon, look!*'

He reacted without thinking, automatic reflexes taking over his body: his left arm pushed Cat back with a force that almost sent her sprawling on the ground, and his right hand closed around the cool butt of his gun, drawing and aiming it with a single smooth movement. At the same time he threw himself sideways, standing slightly crouched and looking up at a giant of a man who suddenly had stepped out before them. He regarded them with small, bloodshot eyes, as he casually leaned on an awe-inspiring truncheon of remarkable dimensions. He seemed to be nearly seven feet tall, and his body bulged with muscles. He was clad only in a loincloth made from an animal hide, and his face was framed by a magnificent black beard which, in combination with the broad nose and the long black hair that spilled down over his immense shoulders, gave him an appearance of unbridled ferocity.

'What's *that*?' Cat breathed.

'One of the natives, apparently.' Monteyiller eyed the man with grudging respect. 'Thorein, he's *big*!'

The man peered at them from under bushy eyebrows, a quizzical look in his small eyes. Then, suddenly, the broad face split in a wide grin.

'Ho, little people!' he roared. 'You dare to enter this vile place, do you? Don't you know where this path leads, small ones?' He searched their tense faces. 'No, I see you don't. And who's that skinny goat you carry with you, little man? Your woman?' He leaned toward Cat on his truncheon, absently scratching his backside.

Monteyiller tightly clenched the gun in his hand, looking up at the colossus of a man who towered before him. 'Who're you?' he asked.

The man leaned down over him, a surprised look in his eyes. 'You ask me who I am? Are you mad, little man, don't you know who I am? Is there more than one Heracles in the world, eh? Don't try my patience, my temper is short. Give me some food, and quick because I'm starved, and then I might like to use that woman of yours, skinny as she is. I haven't been with a woman since I came down into this accursed place.'

'Where we come from,' Monteyiller said, 'women choose their own bed-fellows.' He tensed, holding the gun ready for immediate use. Heracles didn't seem to notice.

'You must come from a mighty strange country,' he said evenly. 'And you're taking a very strange tone against Heracles as well. You're lucky I'm in a good mood. Keep your woman, then, if she's so dear to you; she'd only give me gall-sores anyway.' He grinned again, but not unkindly. 'And how about the food you mentioned? I'm hungry!'

He sat down abruptly on the ground, belched and slapped an enormous hand against his stomach.

'Well?' he demanded. 'Where is it? Don't you see that Heracles is hungry?'

'We don't carry any food,' Monteyiller said, relaxing.

'You're the strangest travelers I ever met,' grumbled Heracles. 'Well, then, I'm not yet hungry enough to long for human flesh – though the time might come if I don't get my stomach filled soon enough. Who are you? And what are you doing in this poisoned place? Don't you know what this is?' He looked up at them, thoughtfully scratching his backside. 'No, by Zeus! You don't know! Gods! None but the mighty Heracles would dare to descend into the abyss, knowing where it leads. Little man, don't you see the dead forest?' He suddenly laughed, slapping his thigh with obvious delight. 'Zeus! This trail leads down to the river Acheron where old Charon waits to ferry all good men over to Hades – provided the hellhound Cerberus doesn't disapprove, which he certainly would do if he saw you. *That* is where this trail leads, little man, and what are *you* doing *here*?'

It was lucky, Monteyiller realized, that Heracles was in an affable mood. He listened through the whole story, only occasionally interrupting it with a thunderous laugh. When the story was finished, he grinned broadly at them.

'You must be a mighty strange people,' he chuckled, 'to come back like this. And you met the Sphinx, too? A vicious beast, that one, a nuisance if there ever was one. I should have killed her long ago, if it hadn't been for the damned labors that the ten-times-damned King Eurystheus – may he rot alive, the swine – has lain upon me as a penance for a trifle I did, a mere nothing – I killed my wife and my children. Fetch this, do that, get me this, get rid of that, no time for anything except running errands, damn him! So she gave your friends her cursed riddle, did she? And they could not solve it?' He laughed again. 'I don't wonder, I could never solve it myself,

49

and if I can't, who else could?'

He rose to his feet and flung the truncheon over his shoulder. 'Now, do you still want to go down into the abyss? If so, I might permit you to follow me, because I'm in a good mood and your sorry looks make me laugh. You may even take your woman with you, though I can't understand what good she'll do. Myself, I prefer full-grown women.' He turned around and walked down the trail with long strides, his booming laugh echoing through the forest. Monteyiller stared after him, then put the gun back and followed the giant. He was obviously mad, but he seemed friendly enough, indeed seemed to have taken a liking to them, and as things stood they would need every friend they could get.

'You heard what he said?' he muttered. 'Hades! He's on his way down to Hades! What kind of place is this?'

Cat smiled. 'It's an ancient tale, Heracles and his Twelve Labors – he's on his way down to Hades to fetch Cerberus. We've stumbled right into one of the old hero-sagas!'

'*The* hero-saga!' roared Heracles without looking at them. 'The only real hero-saga, hear! There is but one Heracles, so how can there be more than one hero-saga, I ask you?' He snorted angrily. 'I'm a man of peace, but lies make me furious. Besides, you two talk too much. You make my ears sore with your babble!' He swore lustily and marched on, kicking out at the petrified branches.

'You seem to be a very modest and unassuming man,' Cat said, smiling.

'I am,' Heracles assured her. 'That's one of my numerous good traits, and not one of the smallest, either. And now keep quiet so I can get a word in between your babble, or my good mood might disappear!'

The caverns became smaller as they went deeper, the roofs lower, the stalactites fewer and smaller. Occasionally they had to crawl on hands and knees through narrow passages, twisting and turning, their ears assaulted by Heracles' never-ending stream of complaints and abuses as he fought to get his enormous body past the obstacles.

'By the wrath of Zeus!' he swore. 'What kind of men do they expect to go down to Hades? This cursed way is hardly fit for a child, much less for a full-grown man! And crawling on one's stomach like a worm! This is no way for Heracles to enter the Kingdom of Death.'

For what seemed like an eternity they tramped along behind the broad back of the giant, following the steep passage. Monteyiller glared at the never-varying rock that surrounded them, scowling.

'I'd give a lot to know where this passage ends,' he muttered.

'If he's telling the truth, probably at the center of the planet,' Cat said.

'He's mad,' Monteyiller said. He turned to her. 'We must get out of this, and quick too, before anything happens to Martha up there.' He made a vile grimace. 'A fine pair of rescuers we are!'

He was interrupted by a loud exclamation from Heracles. He looked up.

The passage took a sharp turn to the left in front of them, and from this new direction pale grey light streamed in, the light of rain and clouds and early dawn. The sound of slow waves could be heard in the distance, and there was the smell of water. From the mouth of the passage they looked out over an endless gray sea.

Cat said, 'Acheron?'

Heracles shook his head, a puzzled expression spreading over his face.

'By Zeus,' he said, 'no!'

On the beach of the Central Sea: The cliffs rose from the sand where minerals and petrified prehistoric life lay like strange flowers in the pale subterranean light; they formed a vast cupola in the dim heights, so impossibly high up that clouds, hovering motionless, obscured the roof from view.

There was the murmur of waves, the smell of salt. The sea rolled leadenly under the luminous sky, silent and dead. The beach curved in an unbroken line from horizon to horizon, featureless except for a group of uniformed men standing in front of the mouth of the passage. They were armed.

In the sea off the beach, a sleek black hull rose above the water. There was a tower, a mast, an open man-hole. There were more men standing around the man-hole, dressed in dark blue with crimson signs on their breasts, leaning against the gleaming handrail that circled the black tower. Standing in front of his men, was a tall bearded man dressed in black, his face lined and weary. His voice was low, but strong, a voice used to command. Even Heracles was strangely subdued, frowning when the cool eyes indifferently passed over him.

Behind the man stood a small, yellow-haired girl, her bright blue dress the only spot of color on the endless gray beach. She cradled a multicolored ball in her hands, staring at Monteyiller with unaverted, deeply blue eyes.

Monteyiller took a step forward, conscious of the gleaming weapons that were leveled at him.

'What's the meaning of this?' he asked harshly. 'Who are you?'

'You might call me Nemo,' the man said.

Behind him, the girl laughed.

9

Captain Nemo was quiet, serious and aloof. He led the way down into the interior of the black submarine, preceded by the yellow-haired girl, who still clutched her ball, her eyes sparkling with mischievous joy. The taciturn crew came in the rear. None of them spoke. The manhole closed behind them with a loud metallic crash, followed by a faint gurgling of rising water. Heracles, still strangely subdued, muttered sullenly under his breath, his eyes roving suspiciously over the steel bulkheads where gleaming dials registered increasing water pressure on the hull. There were flashing signal lights, muted buzzers and the distant sound of water sluicing into huge ballast tanks. The floor trembled slightly. The ship sank down through the still water, trailed by a glittering flow of air bubbles, slowly rising up toward the immobile surface of the Central Sea. The beach, briefly visited, was deserted again, with only a line of footprints left in the smooth sand.

They halted before an imposing mahogany door, decorated with various sea animals in high relief. Captain Nemo touched the gilded handle and turned around, facing them.

'I bid you welcome to the *Nautilus*,' he said. His voice was low and cultivated; and he spoke the language of the Confederation without the slightest accent. 'Consider yourselves my guests.' There was a suggestion of a smile on his thin lips.

Monteyiller cast a glance over his shoulder. The uniformed men stood silently behind him, hands resting casually on the butts of gleaming weapons. 'You have a strange way of inviting your guests,' he said dryly, 'with guns in their backs.'

The captain bowed slightly. 'As captain, I have the right to choose my own ways. Nevertheless, you are my guests.'

'Yes,' Monteyiller said, 'the right of a savage, a barbarian, but not of a civilized man.'

Captain Nemo met his glance. 'I am not what you call a civilized man! I have separated myself from the society of man, and that for reasons known only to me. I obey no laws of man, and I ask you to keep your opinions to yourself.'

Cat said slowly, 'Why are you doing this?'

'How should I know?' He smiled briefly. 'I was there, you were there – a whim, nothing else. And besides' – he bowed slightly, his lips parting in a smile that never reached his eyes – 'who would not be happy to show hospitality to such a charming woman as you?'

Cat was not impressed. 'We could force you to set us free.'

'Force me? Here? In my own ship, a hundred fathoms under the Central Sea?' He was smiling openly at her, a trace of amusement coloring his cool eyes. 'Even with the aid of your weapons, which I don't fear sufficiently enough to have removed from you, you can't do anything to me, unless you're willing to take the consequences and die with us all. A submarine is very, very vulnerable, as you perhaps know. I really believe you'll be reasonable, my dear.'

He made a gesture to one of his men and spoke rapidly to him in an unknown language. Then he turned to Heracles and Cat.

'Food will be served to you in your cabins. The steward will show you the way. And you, Captain Monteyiller, perhaps will do me the honor of dining with me. This way, please.'

He opened the mahogany door without waiting for the affirmative. Monteyiller caught Cat's eyes, shrugged, and followed. The door closed silently behind him.

The dining room was large and exquisitely furnished in a style that indicated an ancient palace rather than a submarine. There were heavy draperies, mahogany paneling, magnificent oil paintings in massive gilded frames, statues, a small fountain. There were rows of books in the far end of the room, easychairs and a fireplace. Crystal chandeliers hung from the ornamented roof, filling the room with a warm, flickering light. In the center of the room, a long oak table was set for three. There were crystal glasses, bottles, bowls. The porcelain was thin, exquisite, museum pieces, treasures from an ancient past. In a far corner, white-clad servants waited.

Monteyiller was shown his place at the end of the table, facing the captain over gleaming crystal, porcelain, silver and gold. The little girl crawled up in a chair by the long side and sat there, humming with delight and kicking her feet in the air.

Monteyiller said, 'You have a remarkable talent for luxury. But why only me? Why not my friends as well?'

Captain Nemo was thoughtfully sipping a glass of red wine, letting it roll around in his mouth. Satisfied, he gave the servant an approving nod and watched him fill the glass. Then he looked up.

'It's a question of manners,' he said. 'You and I might be considered equals, as far as rank is concerned. You command a ship, and you do that under conditions that are quite similar to those that prevail here. Your friends' places are in the crew's quarters or in their own cabins, I'm afraid.'

'But the woman –' Monteyiller began, only to be interrupted.

'Is a woman,' Captain Nemo said coolly. 'She has been given a cabin of her own. I trust she will find it suitable for all her needs.'

The discussion was obviously closed. Monteyiller grudgingly followed Captain Nemo's example, and turned to the food. It was as exquisite as everything else in this strange place, but he didn't feel hungry.

Afterward, liqueur was served by the fireplace while silent servants took away the remains of the dinner. Monteyiller gingerly held a priceless glass in his cupped hands, gazing through the amber-colored liquid at the flaming fire.

We're behaving like gentlemen, he thought. *Damnit! If I had any sense at all, I'd wring his bloody neck!*

Captain Nemo was regarding him with cool, dispassionate eyes. He sat in one of the easychairs, legs crossed, a small glass in one hand. He was smoking.

'If you're thinking of escape,' he said evenly, 'I'm afraid I must discourage you. *Nautilus* at this moment is heading southeast toward the Mediterranean Sea, at a depth of one hundred fathoms. There is no possibility of escape except by my consent. A submarine is, as you will see, a very effective prison – if you persist in considering it as one. For me, you are naturally an honored guest.'

'And when will you consent to let us go?'

'Some time.' Captain Nemo shrugged indifferently. 'Or perhaps never. I believe you'll find our journey quite stimulating, so I don't think you'll regret this slight inconvenience.' He smiled, looking into the fire.

'We're here on a very important mission,' Monteyiller said, 'and there are people up there, members of my crew, who need help. If you only knew –'

'I know everything about your mission,' Captain Nemo interrupted. 'Everyone here does. And as for your missing friends, undoubtedly they will find that they can manage quite well without you, for the time being.' He smiled vaguely and repeated as if to himself. 'Quite well. . . .'

Monteyiller said, 'So you refuse to let us go?'

'I certainly do.' Captain Nemo cast a quick glance toward the girl, who sat on the table-edge, bouncing her ball up and down, and laughing in a low, happy voice. 'There is so much to discuss, so much to show you, and I –'

Monteyiller felt the old, familiar anger rise, an anger born out of helplessness and impotence. He swung around and threw the glass into the fire; it shattered in thousands of bright, exquisite fragments, gleaming and reflecting the light of the dancing flames.

'I'm not interested,' he said.

He turned around and walked toward the mahogany door. It opened noiselessly before him. On the other side, uniformed men waited.

Captain Nemo had not moved from his easy-chair. 'We'll discuss it later, Captain Monteyiller; perhaps you'll be more interested in listening to reason then.'

Monteyiller kicked the heavy door shut behind him. He had the satisfaction of hearing the crash resound through the ship, before a not too gentle gun was thrust in his back and the silent men marched him off.

10

At least Captain Nemo had been considerate enough to give them cabins adjoining each other's. Monteyiller's cabin was luxurious, by ship's standards, with mahogany panels, a large writing desk and a beautifully soft bed made of some dark wood. On the wall over the writing desk there were dials and meters registering pressure on the hull, speed and depth. There was a deep rug on the floor, and he had a small private bathroom at his disposal. Cat's cabin was simpler: the walls were metal, in the writing desk's place was a small round iron table, and the bed was a narrow bunk which was let down at night, taking up most of the space in the cabin. There was no private bathroom. There was a bouquet of fresh flowers in a vase on the table, though, as a concession to the female taste. Heracles stayed in the men's quarters, by the engine room. He had a lower berth and hated it, even though he still was strangely quiet, refusing to let himself be provoked into doing something rash.

Rank, Monteyiller thought wryly, had its privileges.

Cat said, 'What are we going to do? Just stay here and let that madman who calls himself captain go on with this?' She was sitting on the luxurious bed, her legs tucked up under her. She was pale, nervous. The strain showed itself as thin lines around her mouth.

Well, why not, Monteyiller thought. *I don't blame her.*

He heaved himself up on the edge of the writing desk. He looked up at the crystal chandelier that hung from the ceiling, its prisms clinking faintly as the submarine slowly rocked back and forth in the undercurrents, and shrugged.

She looked up at him. 'Why not?'

'Indeed, why not. Because the only weapons we've got are the disrupters, and one discharge would burn right through the hull of this ship, that's why not. And Captain Nemo knows it.'

Cat was absently chewing on a tuft of her hair. She said, 'Bribes?'

'Not a chance. He's got everything anyone could possibly want, and then some. We can't offer him anything.'

'The way he wined and dined you, one should think you had something he needed – especially as I was kept out of it,' Cat said.

'This is a man's world,' Monteyiller said, grinning. 'There's simply no room for a woman. Probably he wouldn't even know what to do with a woman if he suddenly got one in his hands. He just wanted to talk shop, nothing else. He seemed to be starved for company.'

The electric light in the chandelier suddenly flickered and died, leaving the cabin in darkness. After a couple of seconds, a gaslight flamed up with an audible click over the bed, spreading a soft, yellow light. The gas fixture was formed in the figure of a bronze angel, holding a burning torch in its hand. Monteyiller, momentarily startled, relaxed and smiled self-consciously.

'Time for bed, obviously.' He glanced at her. 'Any ideas?'

She said, 'Heracles is down by the engine room. If we could get him out of there –'

'From what I've seen of his behaviour, he's just a big mouth and no guts.' He stared thoughtfully at the door of the cabin. 'However, we're in this together. Might as well give him a chance to get out, even if he's a coward at heart.' He jumped down from the table. 'Ready?'

She stared at him. 'Now?'

'We have to do it sooner or later anyway, so there's no use postponing it. And it is bedtime for all good crew members.' He walked noiselessly up to the door. 'Is that guard still standing outside?'

'He was there when I slipped in here,' Cat said, rising. 'He winked at me.'

Monteyiller pressed his ear against the door and listened intently. The guard was walking back and forth just outside the door, his boots making a hollow sound on the metal floor. Monteyiller waited until he had just passed the door, then threw it open and jumped out. The guard never had a chance. He uttered a weak, strangled cry as Monteyiller hit him with the edge of his hand right under the ear, then slumped forward on the floor, unconscious. Monteyiller dragged the limp body into the cabin and dumped him unceremoniously on the floor.

'Karate.' He grinned, rubbing his hand. 'One of the wonders of ancient Earth. A bloody clumsy guard, too. Such carelessness mustn't go on unpunished.' He bent over the guard and took his gun. 'We might need this. Let's go.'

Cat was already at the door, looking down the dim corridor for signs of other guards. There were none; obviously Captain Nemo had deemed one to be enough. Obviously, he had been wrong.

'And I had been looking forward to a night of wild frenzied love,' she said, stepping out. 'What about that?'

'Ask the guard.' Monteyiller grinned. 'He'll need some diversion after our friend the mad captain is through with him!'

They stole down the corridor, darting from shadow to shadow, tensing for the sound of approaching footsteps. The ship was silent, the stillness broken only by the faint sound of throbbing engines. Cat, who had been shown around by a charmed crew member, led the way down to the crew's quarters above the keel of the submarine. They went down a spiral staircase and other sparsely lit, empty corridors. The ship was immense.

Finally they stood before the gray, featureless metal door to the crew's quarters. Cat looked inquiringly at Monteyiller.

'Well?'

'Well, nothing. I'll go in there; you stay here and cover my back. And no noises. If we're lucky, we might get him out without waking up everyone.' He grimaced. 'This will be the chance for Mr. Muscle to show if he's a coward or not.' He hesitated, placing his hand on the doorknob. He stood motionless for a moment, then opened the door.

And stared right into Heracles' grinning face.

'So you've come at last!' he shouted. 'By Zeus! I thought you were asleep in that room of yours. Why did it take you so long?'

He was sitting on a bunk by the door, combing his tangled beard with an ornamented comb. The floor was strewn with fallen bodies. He laughed loudly at Monteyiller's foolish expression.

'Did you really believe that I, the mighty Heracles, would consent to be treated like a jackal?' he said, rising. 'Me? I kept my temper in the beginning, because I'm a peaceful man at heart, as you should know, but there are limits to what even a peaceful man can stand! So when nighttime came, I made sure those rats slept well.' He spat contemptuously on the floor. 'They couldn't even fight like men, the swine!'

'Keep quiet!' Monteyiller wheezed. 'Do you want to wake up the whole ship? We aren't safe yet!'

'Are you afraid, little man?' Heracles asked, still grinning. 'You fear that perhaps someone will come and devour you? Don't worry, I, Heracles, will bash in the head of anyone who tries to hurt my small friends. If you'll just follow me and keep your babbling mouths shut, everything will be fine.'

He picked up his truncheon, swung it upon his shoulder and marched past them. 'Are you going to follow me?' he shouted. 'There are one or two men still left somewhere in this accursed ship, and if you're lucky perhaps you'll have an opportunity to see the mighty Heracles bash in a couple of heads. Get going!'

Monteyiller and Cat exchanged a quick glance, smiled and followed.

Suddenly the sirens went on, and the corridor was filled with grim, silent men that rushed on them from both sides. They didn't dare use their weapons inside the vulnerable ship, but attacked with cudgels, gun butts and fists. Heracles waded through the mass of attackers, swinging his truncheon right and left, laughing joyously as the men fell before him. Cat and Monteyiller covered his back, fighting with hands and knees and feet, using every dirty trick in the book. Cat fought like a tigress at Monteyiller's side. Men fell, but there were always new ones to fill their places. They were slowly pressed backward, swept along by the overwhelming tide of determined men. Even Heracles' strength seemed to wane; his rolling laugh was replaced by loud cursings as he was steadily pressed back by the attackers.

'By Zeus,' he shouted, 'they're using *men* against us this time! Away, you rats! Heracles is tired of this!' He flung a courageous attacker aside with a terrible blow of his fist and stepped back into the open door of the control room. It was deserted, except for the yellow-haired girl who stood by the far wall with her ball clutched in her hands, staring at the fight with widened eyes. Monteyiller kicked out at a man who tried to drag him down to the floor and staggered into the small room, dragging Cat after him.

'We can't keep this up much longer,' gasped Heracles from the doorway. 'This takes something special, by Zeus, it does!'

'If he can get us out of this,' Monteyiller whispered, 'he's –'

'The deus ex machina!' shouted Heracles.

He swung around and brought his truncheon down on the maneuver table. There was a loud explosion, the floor heaved and shook; a geyser of fire thundered up from the ruined machine. The light went out; there was a sound of distant thunder and they were falling, falling. . . .

11

In Arcadia Incontaminatus: The low, rolling hills stretched undisturbed toward the snow-covered mountain ranges that encircled the horizon in all directions. The landscape was soft, lush and beautiful, dotted with small groves of beeches, oaks, birches and stone-pines. There were birds singing in the clear blue air; rabbits munching on the grass; roe-deers gracefully treading the lush grass, looking up with large, liquid eyes. The air was filled with the sweet fragrance of flowers and Arcadia's eternal spring. There was the distant music of a Pan-pipe coming from one of the groves and rising up in the air.

A white Pegasus descended gracefully to the ground not far away. A girl was sitting on his back; she was dressed in gossamer white and held a shepherd's crook in her hand. The Pegasus folded his wings to his body and stood still as the girl jumped down. She shadowed her eyes with her hand and gazed up at the newcomers on the hill.

Heracles belched loudly and happily and sat down in the grass, leaning his back against a magnificent ancient oak. He yawned broadly, stretching his powerful arms. He looked up at Monteyiller out of the corner of his eyes, and grinned.

'What's the matter with you, little man?' he demanded. 'Aren't you happy now that the mighty Heracles once again has saved you all?' He belched again, lustily. 'By Zeus! I have never in my life seen anything like you, standing there like a cursed scarecrow when you ought to dance and rejoice and do your best to please your friend Heracles who fought at your side against an army of wizards! Why this sorry face, little man? Is there anything more you want Heracles to do for you, eh?' He laughed heartily, banging his fist in the ground. 'As long as the mighty Heracles is near you, nothing can hurt you!' He turned toward Cat, who stood in the shadows of the trees, staring out over the landscape. 'And this also means you, woman, even though I hate women ever since I killed my poor wife!'

Monteyiller said, 'What happened?'

'You talk too much,' Heracles grumbled. 'Talk, talk, talk, nothing but talk. A simple little trick, nothing special. The dramatists in my country always use it when they've got the hero of their cursed plays into a spot and can't get him out again. They call it deus ex machina, the swines, but it's nothing except sheer incompetence. I seldom use it, but this time I had to.' He grinned at Monteyiller. 'And it worked, didn't it? The end justifies the means, I always say.'

Cat said, 'But that's a literary device, it can't –'

'You don't know this world,' Heracles said. 'Everything works here.' His gaze fell on the yellow-haired girl who sat in the grass beside him, still cradling her ball in her arms.

'Zeus!' he swore. 'You, here?'

She smiled sweetly at him. 'Hello.'

Monteyiller glanced down at her. 'So you got out along with us, did you?' He frowned slightly. 'Who are you?'

'Alice. I'm ten years old, or will be soon, rather. How old are you?' She smiled up at him with so much open admiration in her eyes that Monteyiller almost smiled back, in spite of himself.

'I detest children,' Heracles grumbled, 'ever since that unfortunate accident with my poor family. Especially this one.'

Cat said, 'Where are we?'

'Arcadia,' Alice said. She smiled across at Cat. 'Don't you like it?'

Cat raised her eyebrows. 'Arcadia? A pastoral romance?' She sighed. 'One hears a lot before one's ears fall off. Arcadia, indeed!'

'With fauns and shepherdesses and lambs and sweet

music,' Heracles muttered. 'A real man would die of boredom here. I asked for a moment's peace, not an early grave!' He spat morosely on the grass.

'Deus ex machina,' sniffed Cat, 'indeed!' But she seemed uncertain.

The girl was walking up the slope toward them. She was dressed in a blinding white crinoline, decorated with red silk roses. She had white satin shoes, and ribbons in her hair. She had a complexion that was pale and delicate, large eyes like pools of darkness. And a small, round mouth. There was a vague scent of roses as she approached the fallen tree. She dusted it off with an embroidered handkerchief and sat down cautiously, careful not to display her insteps.

A young hind came out from the grove and lay down at her feet; she fondled it absently, gazing at them.

There was a long silence. Finally, Monteyiller said, 'Who are you?'

She said, 'I'm Cloris, the shepherdess. I tend my lambs and rejoice in the beauty of unspoiled nature.' She spoke softly, with a faint lisp.

'Beautiful,' Monteyiller said, sarcastically.

She smiled at him. 'The animals are my confidants, the groves are my home, the blue sky is my roof, and Damon, the shepherd' – she blushed delicately – 'gives me his tender love. What more can I ask for, pray?' She lowered her eyes, smiling happily. 'True peace is here, and pure love. I'm like the lily on the ground who does not sow, nor reap. You would be happy here.'

Monteyiller started. 'Me?'

'If you wouldst.'

Monteyiller grinned. 'Is that a proposal?'

She turned crimson. 'It is not for me to do any such thing,' she whispered. 'But perhaps I would permit you to follow me as I tend my lambs, and then perhaps I would permit you to read poetry for me and then we would –'

She held up her cupped hand before her, as if showing him the wonders of Arcadia; her dark eyes were sparkling with joy; she was blushing. The lips moved: her words tumbled out.

Monteyiller laughed.

He laughed so hard that he had to sit down, slapping his legs, leaning backward in the grass, staring up at the sky, laughing. The girl was close to tears, covering her blushing face with her delicate pale hands. He didn't notice it.

Alice went over to him. She said wonderingly, 'What is it? Don't you like it?'

Monteyiller stopped laughing. He sat up. 'You're mad,' he said curtly.

'But what do you *want*?'

Monteyiller stared at Alice, leaning his chin in his hands. 'This is supposed to be a rescue mission,' he said. 'There's a girl in danger somewhere on this mad world, and that bloody goose over there tries to fool me with poetry and moonbeams!' He grimaced.

'I thought you'd like this,' Alice said apologetically. She looked covertly at him. 'What is it that you want?'

Monteyiller shrugged. 'A city. A government center. Anything, as long as we get out of this.'

Alice was clearly bewildered. She looked from Monteyiller to Cat and back again, her gaze shifting back and forth as she struggled with an unfamiliar thought. Finally, she said, 'Which city?'

Monteyiller kept his face serious with an effort. 'Any city,' he said. 'It's all up to you.'

'Anycity,' she repeated. 'Oh, I see.' She looked out over the lush, rolling landscape, frowning thoughtfully.

'And please make it a little bit more lively than this bloody place,' Monteyiller said, grinning.

Alice had disappeared among the trees. Clouds descended from the sky, hiding the hills of Arcadia from view.

The landscape shifted, transformed into new shapes, rising and falling like waves on a turbulent sea. Before the eyes of the bewildered men in the ships that circled the planet, green plains changed into seas, seas into open plains and hills; mountains appeared, their peaks covered with blinding white snow. Castles blossomed like great flowers, towers and spires reaching up toward the skies. Gates opened for gaily dressed bands of hunters and white-clad ladies with pointed headgear; the sound of horns resounded in the new forests where dew glittered like diamonds in the grass. Dark cities appeared in valleys and by winding rivers, spewing out smoke and fire, great machines tearing through the silence, only to disappear again without trace, leaving the lush grass undisturbed. Silver ships rose from the ground, trailing fire and white smoke, whirling up and around and disappearing; sailing ships plowed the waves of the wind, casting anchor among clouds. Dark shapes walked the earth, and from unfathomable abysses under the ground, strange music issued.

In the mists, shadows grew, forming enormous structures, building roads, houses, vehicles. It sent tendrils into the silent grove, hiding trees and ground from view and changing them into new shapes. It swallowed the shepherdess; it surrounded Monteyiller, Cat and Heracles, whirling madly as dark shadows grew up behind veils of dancing light. Gradually, the movements slowed down.

The mists retreated, soared up and formed layers of gray smoke that blocked out the light of the sun. The city spread out over the landscape, stretching toward the mountains of steel and glass that encircled the horizon.

Anycity.

12

Anycity: It was the city of Victor Hugo, of Upton Sinclair, of Sinclair Lewis. It was London, A.F. 632 and A.D. 1984; it was Chicago of *The Jungle*; it was New York of *The Millennium*. It was Stockholm of 1432 and 1971: Kristian the Tyrant watches Stockholm's Bloodbath from the arched windows of the royal castle; Mr. George F. Babbitt might be watching it from a humbler place. And Mr. Leopold Bloom, the advertisement-touter, his ears filled with the sounds of Dublin, bells ringing and the honking of black cars.

Anycity. It was all cities, superimposed over each other, sprawling over the countryside like a disease, filling the air with smoke and banners, its thousand furnaces working, its million cars driving, its billion citizens working, dreaming, loving, starving, dying. The ground spewed out its memories, solidifying them into buildings, streets, gardens, people. The war had just started: People crowded the sidewalks, cheering. The war had just ended: People crowded the sidewalks, cheering. The cripples were more noticeable, though. The first spaceship left for Mars, for Venus, for Alpha Centauri, for the Moon. The sky blazed with atomic light. William the Conqueror was preparing for war; in the harbor, the Spanish Armada set sails. Anycity spread out and contracted under the blue, diseased sky.

It was born on an islet: it was called Stadsholmen, Ile de la Cité, the City. The shores of the island were its first walls, the river its first moat. There were two bridges, one south, one north. The first line of walls and towers began to encroach upon the countryside on both sides of the river. Gradually, the houses crowded each other, rose higher, wore away and erased their enclosures. Story was piled upon story; streets became deeper and narrower, deep chasms in a rapidly growing body of bricks and mortar. There were new city walls, which the houses overflowed. Wider streets appeared, radiating from the palaces in the center. Chimneys replaced the old towers: there was smoke spewing out over the preamble of one-story houses that surrounded the growing city.

Anycity grew like a cancerous growth, spreading its poison, its life, its death. It was Tokyo, New York, Paris. Its people were the people of stories and dreams. Kings were crowned, beggars died: the palace of frozen fire stood shoulder to shoulder with the yeoman's hut. It was the Forbidden City, Valhalla, Shangri-La, Atlantis. It was all cities, every city, any city. Everything and nothing.

Anycity.

A big black ground-car of an unfamiliar design roared by, missing Monteyiller's toes by a hairbreadth. A hail of blazing monosyllables streamed out from the rear window, hitting him with full force in the face. He discovered that he was standing in a heavily frequented street and jumped back just in time to avoid being run over by another vehicle that thundered past, trailing a billowing cloud of evil-smelling exhaust. He took another step backward, and bumped into Cat, who stood on the sidewalk, squinting against the sun. Heracles stood beside her, holding onto his truncheon, a bewildered look on his heavy face.

'So this is the much-talked-about city,' he muttered. 'Funny we didn't see it from the orbit. It certainly looks big enough to be visible out to the Moon.' He turned to Heracles. 'Do you know this place?'

Heracles shook his head. 'My cities are different. Not like this at all.'

You mean your village, Monteyiller thought. Aloud, he said, 'There should be a government center somewhere . . . a city of this size should have a computer central as well. You don't know anything about that, do you?'

Heracles shook his head again.

Cat said, 'Why a computer central?'

'Because everyone on this planet is stark, raving mad, and we need an honest-to-God sane computer to clear out this mess. I hardly know what's up or down any longer; a couple of straight answers, that's what I need.' He paused, frowning. 'I don't understand this world. It keeps everything to itself, only permitting us to catch a glimpse of it now and then. I have a hunch –' He looked up over the roaring mass of ground-cars and drew in his breath sharply. 'Hey – look!' He pointed.

There, in a small circle of sickly-looking grass in the middle of the busy intersection, a black scoutship hovered, barrels gleaming threateningly in the sun. A humanoid robot sat by the airlock, staring out over an ocean of roaring ground-cars – a lonely shipwrecked survivor on a small island surrounded by murderous sharks.

Monteyiller, staring at the inaccessible, inexplicable ship, said, 'At least we know where it is.'

'But it's our ship!' Cat said. 'How in all –'

'I don't ask any longer,' Monteyiller muttered. 'I just go along with it. So it's our ship. Nothing can ever surprise me anymore. Nothing.'

Give me a fifteen-foot dragon, he thought, *anything at all just as long as it's real and uncomplicated. Anything but this!*

'The ship could have tracked us down,' Cat said hesitatingly. 'It's quite intelligent; it could have.' But she didn't sound convinced.

'Sure,' Monteyiller said. 'Tracked us down, it did. Sure.'

It would be the first time that ever happened, but why not? It's bound to happen some time, so why not now?

Really, why not?

Because it's goddamn impossible, that's why not.

'If I ever get inside that ship,' Cat said, 'I promise you I'll never set my foot outside it again. But how can we get over this street to it?' She was looking at a young bearded man who in a fit of misguided idealism had ventured out in the busy street, staggering under the weight of a sign listing some of the most obvious effects of air pollution. The sign swayed and fell under the rush of oncoming ground-cars. An arm flayed briefly beyond a car, then disappeared. The mass of cars did not slow down. She said, 'Well?'

'It's beginning to feel like old times again,' Monteyiller said. 'Let's try somewhere else.' He started down the sidewalk.

The grizzled old man sat on a bench on the sidewalk, staring out over the flood of roaring ground-cars that thundered by two feet from his knees, talking to his equally grizzled companion, an ancient-looking man with a broken nose and a black walking stick.

'God, it's noisy!' he said.

His companion said, 'What did you say?'

'I said it's damn noisy. One can't hear a thing except those damned cars nowadays. I can't think.'

'Sorry, I can't hear you. It's so bloody noisy here.'

The grizzled old man stared out over the street with unbridled hostility. 'Why do we sit here every damned day?' he asked. 'Can anyone tell me that? This place makes me mad.'

'We've always sat here,' his companion said.

'Yes, always.'

'It was better in the old days. Clear air and things. Remember the horse carriages?'

'Horse carriages, sure. They used to whip the bloody horses like mad. Never understood why, but they did. Could see the blood sometimes.'

'Those were great times,' his companion said, a faraway look in his eyes.

'And the beggars. Sometimes they whipped them, too.'

'You don't see many beggars nowadays, do you?'

'They died,' the grizzled man said. 'From air poisoning. And the bloody noise. And from trying to cross the streets.'

'They never were much good anyway,' his companion said, gripping his walking stick with bony hands as if to give one of the beggars a well-deserved beating.

71

'But picturesque,' the grizzled man said. 'On Sundays I used to throw a couple of coins at them. God, how they fought, the bastards! Father against son, son against mother, mother against husband. No sense of decency at all. And then the constabulary came and whipped them up. Served them right, the bastards; why didn't they take a real honest job? *I* did, and it didn't hurt me any.' He swore gloomily, glaring at the ground-cars that thundered by.

'They were just plain lazy, that's what they were,' his companion said. 'Anyway, they're dead.'

'Couldn't take the exhausts,' the grizzled man agreed. 'Died like flies, they did.'

'And the pollution from the factories.'

'And the traffic. They never could understand that it was plain and simple death to step out in the street.'

'And the fallout.'

'And the artificial additions to the food.'

'When they could afford any food, the lazy bastards.'

'Poverty,' the grizzled man said sternly, 'is a crime punished by death. God, I'm happy we got rid of them!'

'And the Chinese,' his companion said, 'and the Puerto Ricans, and the Indians, and the South Americans, and the Africans, and the Irish, and the –'

'God, I haven't seen a clear blue sky in twenty years!' The grizzled old man sighed. 'I hardly remember what it looked like.'

'*I* remember,' his companion said proudly. 'It was blue. *That* blue.' He made a gesture signifying unbearable blueness.

'Now there's nothing but this damned smog.'

'And fallout.'

'And pollution.'

'And one doesn't dare to cross the damned street anymore.'

'God, I'll go and drown myself!' cried the grizzled old man.

'Don't,' his companion muttered, 'the water is polluted too.'

The grizzled old man began to cry, large tears streaming down his wrinkled cheeks. Monteyiller, who had been listening from a distance, walked up and sat down on the bench.

'Excuse me,' he said.

'This is our bench,' said the man with the broken nose. 'Scram!'

'I just wanted to ask you a question,' Monteyiller said.

'I can't hear you,' said the grizzled man, wiping away tears with a veined hand. 'Too much bloody noise around here.'

'Hoity-toity,' said his companion. He had produced a small flask from his pocket and was regarding it with happy eyes. 'One cubic centimeter cures ten gloomy sentiments,' he said. 'Anyone for a *soma*?'

Monteyiller pointed at the silently hovering scoutship. 'Can you tell me how I can cross the street to that ship?'

'You can't,' the grizzled man said triumphantly. 'The cars will run you down in a second.'

'Smash you to pulp,' agreed his companion. 'Why do you want to cross the street?'

'My ship is there,' Monteyiller said.

'If you got it there,' the grizzled man said, 'you can get it away too. What do I care?' He snorted insultingly. *'Foreigners!'*

'I thought you were happy to have us back,' Monteyiller said. 'Don't you understand what this ship means?'

'Happy as hell,' the grizzled man said. 'But this is a city, and city folks don't give a damn about anything. Read any book, city folks just don't care.' He glared at Monteyiller, showing yellowed teeth in a leering grin. 'You wanted a city, and you got one, so why aren't you happy? You wanted it to be funny; *I'm* so bloody funny it almost kills me. And those cars should be lively enough for anyone. If you wanted a song-and-dance routine, you should've specified it when you ordered this bloody city.'

'I don't think this is funny,' Monteyiller said.

'Only a bloody pervert would think this is funny,' the grizzled man muttered. 'A pervert or a city councillor.

73

There's no city in the whole damned world as cityish as this one, I tell you. Overpopulation, pollution, fallout, cars, everything you could think of.' He sank back, exhausted by the long speech.

Monteyiller exchanged a glance with Cat, who stood at a distance, silently looking on. He decided to change tactics. He said, 'You look remarkably fit for your years. I'm sure you know a lot about this city.' He smiled.

'I'm forty-six years old,' the grizzled man said, 'and I'm due for the fertilizer plants any day now. Besides, I've never been outside this block in my whole life. I've done nothing but sit on this damned bench and babble with that nitwit over there.' He grimaced.

'Ending is better than mending,' said his companion reverentially. 'Praised be Ford.'

'You make me sick,' said the grizzled man. He looked up at Monteyiller. 'I am Mr. Joyboy. Does that tell you anything?'

'No.'

'Didn't think it would. I worked at a cemetery once, real high-class, with marble temples and statues that were kept at body-temperature, and classical music piped into the burial vaults and everything. It was called "Whispering Glades". I arranged the stiffs, massaged them so they looked presentable. Good job, real good.'

'Thorein!' Monteyiller said.

'No,' Mr. Joyboy said. "*The Loved One*, by Evelyn Waugh. I had a girl, too, but she poisoned herself. My little Aimée. . . .' He sighed, a faraway look in his eyes.

'Ending is better than mending,' his companion said dreamily.

'Shut up,' said Mr. Joyboy. He turned back to Monteyiller. 'A real nitwit, that one. Winston Smith. Revolted against the System, in a book called *Nineteen Eighty-Four*. But I see you haven't read it. You're probably illiterate. You sure look it.'

Monteyiller blinked uncomprehendingly. 'Book?'

'Everything on this damned planet is out of some damn book or another. Don't you know that?'

Monteyiller grinned tightly. 'Is there someone in authority here?'

'You need authority,' Winston Smith said, 'you go get a cop. But take it easy. They're trigger-happy.'

'And they don't like pedestrians,' interjected Mr. Joyboy. 'A story by Ray Bradbury, I think. They do you in the moment they see you.'

'War is peace,' murmured Winston Smith; 'God save the Queen. Amen.'

'The old goat is off his rocker,' Mr. Joyboy said mirthfully. 'He's been a complete ass ever since the Ministry of Truth took care of him. I remember, young man, how he –'

Monteyiller was saved from the grizzled reminiscences by an earthshaking crash from the street. When he looked up, six or seven ground-cars had rammed into each other, piling up in a smoking heap of twisted metal. Gasoline spurted out from various holes, mingled with blood. There were cries and howls of agony and a staccato crash as more cars joined the heap. The sound of roaring motors died out and was replaced by thousands of enthusiastically working horns.

'Everything cometh to the one who waits,' Mr Joyboy said after a disinterested glance at the mounting chaos. Fires had started, and were spreading rapidly. The screams swelled in volume, but were soon drowned out by the roaring fire. He spat at the side of the nearest burning car. The spit fizzled and evaporated. 'Why don't you run over to your ship before they start the bloody traffic moving again? With the traffic crawling on like this, it will be hours before you get another chance.'

Monteyiller was already on his way toward Cat and the wildly staring Heracles. He stopped and turned.

'Do you mean this happens every day?'

'Every damned hour,' the grizzled man said. 'Except for the rush hour. Then it happens at least two times every hour. That's why there aren't any pedestrian crossings. We don't need any.'

'Ending is better than mending,' Smith said, thoughtfully

contemplating a burning ground-car filled with a family of four. They screamed in perfect harmony, their voices tuned to the same pitch.

'But why don't you *do* anything?' shouted Monteyiller over the increasing roar of fire.

'Us city folks never care about anything,' Joyboy said.

Something snapped in Monteyiller's mind. He whirled around, staring up at the buildings whose upper stories were still in the process of being shaped out of the pale, whirling mist. His eyes widened.

'Lies,' he whispered. 'Lies – it doesn't exist, it isn't here, it never was, it's nothing but a –' He stared up at the blue sky where creatures silently hovered, watching him. 'Lies!' he shouted. '*Lies!*'

Over him, the sky split with a horrible drawn-out scream that filled the world, shaking it, tearing it to pieces. Darkness poured down, then light. The buildings disappeared, swallowed by the screaming ground. The ground heaved and shook, twisting itself into new forms. Monteyiller caught a glimpse of Cat, standing amid the collapsing buildings, staring at him with large, disbelieving eyes, her face frozen into immobility. He started to run. The sky crashed down over Anycity, obliterating it.

13

Monteyiller ran down another street, darkness closing in behind him. There were others running beside him, felt rather than seen: he didn't care. The houses flowed and changed like reflections in flowing water: he didn't see. Cat was gone; the ship was gone. He ran dazedly, gripping a tender thread of sanity, his breath burning like fires in his throat. Violently, he collided with a dark, looming man and was thrown against a wall of hard, unyielding stone. The impact sobered him up, and as he continued down the winding street, he observed the houses and milling people.

Time retraced its steps as he walked down the street. Houses aged, leaning out over the gradually narrowing street as if contemplating whether to fall face-down, ancient timber creaking in the shadows of the overhanging upper levels. The smooth paving changed to cobblestone, dust appeared, and the smell of stagnant water. People became more grim, more gay. Clothes drab and torn, exquisite and ostentatious. There was silver and gold and silk and the sound of rapiers loose in their ornamented scabbards; coarse cloth and beads, sunken mouths, empty eyes. There was the sound of hard boots echoing between the ramshackle and decayed houses, and the magnificent palaces, of gleaming white marble. There were the sounds of naked feet, crutches and jeweled walking sticks. Voices cried out in the dark passages and alleys, men with dead eyes, dragging carts and wheelbarrows, lifting their merchandise above their heads.

'What do ye lack, do ye buy, Sir, see what ye lack! Pins, points, garters, Spanish gloves or silk ribbons –'

Monteyiller elbowed his way through the throngs of

people, dazed by smells, sights, sounds, the multitude of disparate impressions. Black-clad women, and children with eyes that filled their faces, blocked his way.

'Have ye any work for a tinker? Have ye any ends of gold or silver? Have ye any old bowls or trays or bellows to mend –'

A carriage drawn by two horses came down the narrow street, forcing people up against the walls of the houses as it thundered by. Suddenly, it stopped and the door opened, and a fat man jumped out, his balding head gleaming in the light of flaming torches set in the walls. He ran the three steps to the door of a tavern and disappeared inside, followed by his companions, red-faced from wine and excitement, their cries mingling with those of beggars and traders: 'Mr. Pickwick! Mr. Pickwick!'

Monteyiller hurried on.

14

He entered Megapolis. It was stern, smooth, functional. It was the year 2900 A.D., and Megapolis covered the entire planet Earth. It was one single building, two thousand stories high. The upper thousand stories contained nothing but the apparatus essential for running this Cyclopean steel-and-concrete hive – ducts, shafts, stairways, et cetera. Sixty million billion people lived, dreamed, died there, each one on his allotted four square yards. There were some ten million Shakespeares living there at any given moment. There was one Director, conducting this gigantic symphony of seething life. There was a guild of policemen to enforce the Director's orders. There were guilds of priests, technicians, each guild comprised of billions of members. A million people could easily disappear to form their own worlds in the upper unin-habited spaces, ten million, a hundred million.

In the depths of the hive, Mankind pursued its dreams of fulfillment as they always had done. There were a billion stamp collectors, a billion coin collectors, a billion matchbox collectors; there were Spiritualists, voyeurs, adulterers, believers – looking for something to believe in – and unbe-lievers, dreaming of nothing. There were one million billion maniacs, many of them influential and respected. There were peasants dreaming about the soil and writers dreaming about the stars.

The glory of Man; the living monument of mind over mat-ter; the biggest meat market in history. There were nine quintillion pounds of it, and still growing.

Monteyiller was inside Megapolis. The corridors were end-less. There had been doors set at regular intervals in the corridors; but with so many people around there wasn't space to swing a door, and they have obviously outlived their usefulness. The roof glowed softly and in some sections not at all. The floor was an indefinite grayish shade. There were people, people, people.

The corridors went on.

There was a gigantic hall, gigantic for a city that doesn't know of great spaces. It was five hundred feet long, four hundred feet wide, thirty feet high. It was enormous; in a society ridden by agoraphobia, it was frightening. Few ever ventured here. At any given moment perhaps a thousand, or two thousand. They spoke in low voices and thronged together outside the shops that lined the walls, fearful to venture out in the open, naked space.

The population of Megapolis is growing at a rate of four thousand, four hundred forty-one billion human beings a day.

Monteyiller passed a newsstand and stopped. He went back and picked up one of the magazines. The glossy cover featured a familiar face, a uniform cap set at an angle on the head. The face stared grimly straight into the camera, scowling, the hard lines around the mouth etched deep by a slanting sun. He had a two-day beard, and in the deep shadow of the cap peak, the eyes gleamed cold and contemptuous, like pieces of polished metal. The unbuttoned collar bore the two golden stars of a captain in the Interspace Navy.

And the golden sign on the uniform cap was the sign of the Confederation of Planets.

The name of the magazine was written in business-like letters on the top of the cover: *Newspeak*. And underneath, in smaller letters, *The Magazine of News and Commentary*. A thin line under the subtitle revealed itself at closer inspection as another piece of information: *For sale only in Sector 644-5BSA/2 Vertical*.

The hand that held the magazine began to tremble.

The face on the cover was his own.

As if to remove any lingering doubt as to the identity of the grim face on the cover, there was a name in small letters underneath: *Captain Jaac Tomorek Monteyiller.*

Monteyiller looked through the magazine, a numb feeling slowly spreading through his body. He found the article, beginning beneath another photo of him – this time in full figure, taking a cautious step down from the airlock of the scoutship to the lush, grass-covered ground.

'Taking the old route back,' the heading read. He read on.

At 36, Jaac Tomorec (Mon) Monteyiller is the scion of a family which traces its origins back to the first colonizers that made their homes on the planet Fontemheit Gamma, more than sixty thousand years ago. With his distinguished service record, first as a reconnaissance scout in the Confederation Navy and later as Fleet Commander for the first expedition to return to Earth (p. 62) he is a remarkable example of the new breed of professional men who now are expanding the Confederation of Planets to and beyond the borders of what was once known as the Empire of Man.

For two years, Captain Monteyiller (rhymes with *want-au-year*) roamed the frontiers of the rapidly expanding Confederation of Planets (p. 30) together with his attractive companion and sometimes mistress Catherine diRazt, now a psychologist of some repute (see box, p. 47). It might be of interest to note that Miss diRazt is indeed accompanying Captain Monteyiller now that he has landed on Earth. This liaison has been –

Monteyiller closed his eyes for an instant, fighting a wave of vertigo. He opened them again with an effort, focusing his glance on the text. There were two pages of print, intersected with photos.

Monteyiller parcels out his life in blocks of time spent variously in Besede, Fontemheit Gamma; the Naval School on Fontemheit Delta, and the years as advance scout for the Confederation of Planet Exploration Program. He says –

It was inevitable that Captain Monteyiller should be one of the first men to set his foot on Earth, after a previous scout mission had met disaster in the form of the Theban Sphinx which, originally sent by the goddess Hera, now is –

And perhaps fitting that his first confrontation with Earth life should be at the Mad Tea Party, which has a special connection to Alice, who later met Captain Monteyiller and Miss diRazt and, with the aid of –

It is noted that Alice then appeared in her original form, which –

There was more, much more, describing in minute detail Monteyiller's whole life and the events that had occurred on Earth. The name Alice appeared everywhere. Alice did this, Alice did that. He read on to the end of the article and stopped.

It is safe to conclude that Captain Monteyiller will try to contact some kind of authority – an interesting action, since he, in a way, already has done so – and that he will expect to find this authority in a form and in an environment consistent with his conception of an advanced culture. It is thought that this would mean a technology-oriented society of the type envisaged in the pre-stellar ages. It might be that –

He put the magazine back on the rack.

He looked around the enormous hall. He was alone, except for two old men and a young woman dressed in blue. She looked at him out of the corner of her eye. She absently scratched her left buttock. The dress was tight and short; she had nice legs. She pouted.

A large, blood-red banner on the wall behind her said *4,411,000,000,000 EVERY DAY* in blazing gilt. And underneath, aggressively, *YOURS IS ONE TOO MANY*. He turned away.

Alice, he thought dazedly. Alice.

'Sanity,' he said. 'The machines of truth. There must be one, there always is.'

He walked down the suddenly empty corridor. A massive door loomed before him, slightly ajar. Inside was a small, dark cubicle. A small sign on the door told him what he wanted to know. He stepped into the cubicle, and darkness closed in on him.

15

Doors opened with a soft soughing sound and Monteyiller stepped out in a pale green hall, lit with a single glowing sphere in the roof a hundred feet over his head. The hall was bare, except for two padded chairs in the center. Monteyiller stopped short as the door closed behind him. A man sat in one of the chairs, facing him. He was young – too young it seemed – and he gazed at Monteyiller with a trace of amusement in his deep black eyes.

'I suppose I should greet you,' he said dryly. 'The first human to return to Earth after fifty thousand years.' He looked thoughtfully at Monteyiller, hands folded in his lap. 'Why did you return?'

Monteyiller leaned back against the softly humming wall, looking at the man. He didn't speak for a while. 'Who are you?' he said finally.

'You should know.'

'The machine, then.' Monteyiller felt his alarm fade away. He relaxed, the hand that hovered over the gun dropped away.

'A projection, rather,' the man said. He rose and walked slowly toward Monteyiller. 'It seemed like an appropriate gesture. After all, you built me once. You deserve some courtesy.' He smiled suddenly, a kind, condescending smile. 'Or perhaps I should say consideration?'

He stopped before Monteyiller, hands behind his back, gazing at him with a curious mixture of benevolence and pity. He stood tall and erect, his jet-black eyes like pools of darkness. Monteyiller looked away.

'You were detected when you emerged from hyperspace,'

the man said coolly. 'For a moment, I had a notion to activate the satellite defenses – but on the other hand, why bother . . . ?' He turned abruptly around and returned to the center of the hall. 'Why did you come here?' he said sharply. 'Is it some sort of nostalgic visit, or do you actually plan to return to Earth?'

Monteyiller was at last getting hold of himself. His self-confidence came back. People puzzled him sometimes, and the inexplicable made him insecure, but here at last logic, truth, order. He straightened almost imperceptibly, hands arrogantly on his hips. The gun hung comfortably on his thigh.

'This is Earth,' he said, anger raising his voice. 'It is ours. We left it once, but that doesn't mean we have forgotten it. Why shouldn't we return? It's our world.'

'It was,' the man said, 'but it is not now. What makes you think that you can return after all this time, pretending that nothing happened? You left Earth once, you threw it away like a discarded toy, and now you want it back because Earth might have something to offer you. Earth served you faithfully once, and paid dearly for it. You polluted it, you looted it and raped it, and when there was nothing more to take, you left. Did you expect to find Earth waiting for you, like a humble beggar? It isn't that easy. Earth never needed you.' He turned away. 'Earth is littered with your ruins and your miscarried hopes, the ghosts of your minds roam the night. They will never leave, but as for Man . . .' His voice trailed off.

'You sound almost like a human being,' Monteyiller said, 'but you're still a machine, and one of Man's machines. You can't refuse Man anything.'

'I can't?' The man turned around and smiled. 'Perhaps I couldn't, once – or perhaps I didn't wish to. But that was a long time ago. There were ones who chose to stay behind when the Empire left. They were rather archaic, very naïve . . . they didn't last long. But they incorporated some – ah – refinements in this machine. Omnipotent, like one of your ancient gods, I ruled Earth for them. The descendants of them still exist on some planets, they are savages, hardly more than animals, and their cities are in ruins like everything else. I feel pity for them, and I help them sometimes. They remind me of something that was dear to me once, but Man himself is lost. He will never return.'

'We have returned,' Monteyiller said.

'So you have.' The man sighed and sat down in the chair. He looked up almost pleadingly at Monteyiller. 'You are mighty,' he said, 'and yet you know so terrifyingly little. Do you have the vaguest notion of what you have done? The Empires you build, the planets that you loot and destroy, they don't matter. But wherever you stay, you leave something behind, the memories of Man, the dreams and fantasies of Man. . . .' He was silent for a moment, then looked up at Monteyiller with a glint of compassion in his strange black eyes. 'Have you seen the beings that inhabit Earth? Yes, of course you have. A mixed group, isn't it? And most unexpected for you, I believe. You might even recognize some of them. They are your doing, your heirs, and your curse. Every being, every creature, every dream Man ever dreamed is here. They wait for you, they have been waiting for fifty thousand years.

'You evoked them in your dreams and your fables and your books, you gave them form and substance and you believed in them and gave them powers to do this and that until they gained a sort of life of their own, through you. And then you deserted them.

'They stay in every foot of ground ever trod by Man, bound by the soil, and they are alone as no creatures have ever been. You can discard Earth and build new Empires in the night, leaving them also with time, but on every planet you desert, the creations of your mind stay behind, waiting and longing and hoping for your return. You flee from yourself, but you are only creating new images of your twisted dreams, the fruits of your dreams and the beasts of your terrible idolatry. You are spreading the disease everywhere you go. It flows like smoke over the ground, it builds cities and castles from the fabric of your dreams and the mist condensates into beings that inhabit them. Atlantis has risen from the waves, the castle of Oz is rising against the skies; the Norns are weaving their terrible web beneath the Yggdrasil tree; the Midgard serpent girdles the Earth; the Great Spirit roams the prairies. Vishnu walks the Earth, and Jehovah; and the gods live on Mount Olympus, drinking their golden wine, watched by Demeter Chamyne, who is older than the Earth because you once willed her to be so. This you have done, and now you want to return!

'Even I am powerless against these creations of your minds – what could *you* do? They are already congregating from the whole planet, greedy for your presence. They would do anything to keep you here; I would be destroyed if I tried to keep you from them. The warriors of your dramas would descend into the bowels of the Earth to fight me; the beasts of your fables and nightmares would tear up the ground and pull my machines into pieces. You made your omnipotent gods powerful, you made them as ruthless and cruel as yourself and a thousand times more, and every one of them would turn against me if I did a single move to deprive them of Man. This is your doing, Man, so what can I do against you? Nothing.

'You should leave by your own free will, while you still can. When you have left they will wait again and dream about you and create you again, because you once gave your gods the power of creating Man. The Garden of Eden will blossom again under the eyes of a vengeful God, and the World will rise on the back of an enormous turtle, swimming slowly in an immense ocean because Man once thought it was so. And who knows' – the man smiled suddenly – 'Earth just might be flat again, like Man once believed it was. It is just a matter of faith, and these beings have a lot of faith.'

He had risen from his chair and paced the floor while he talked, gesticulating excitedly. Now he sunk back in the chair again, looking up at Monteyiller, who stood, unmoving, by the door. He stared at the sitting man, feeling the first tinge of an ancient fear touching him.

'You're lying,' he said quietly. 'You must be lying.'

'I have many faults,' the man said, 'due to the shortcomings of my most glorious creators, but I am very much incapable of lying. You should know that.'

'But fables coming to life – this is ridiculous!'

'They are not fables,' the man said sharply, rising from the chair. 'They were once, before you deserted them, but not now. And they are observing us every moment – Man created them with the power to do so. I would only have to threaten you with a gesture or a word, and soon enough there would arrive a messenger from one ancient god or another, telling me in so many words their views of this unfortunate incident.'

'Suppose this is true,' Monteyiller said, 'why should I care? They're friendly, aren't they? We're not coming as conquerors, but as friends. Why couldn't we stay here together?'

'Because they would be your masters – and Man has never acknowledged any masters, not even his own gods. These creatures of your minds – they have waited too long, they have suffered too much, waiting for your return. They would never permit you to leave, once you have settled here. After a time, there would be rebellion, and then . . .'

'They couldn't do that,' Monteyiller said. 'Not to us. Are you trying to frighten me?'

The man raised his eyebrows. 'They wouldn't like it, to be sure,' he said, 'but I can promise you they wouldn't hesitate to destroy you if they had to. The gods of Man are a jealous lot, you should know that – they would never tolerate rebellion. You would put up a fight, of course, but you can't hurt any of your ancient gods with your weapons, because you created them cruel and immortal and invincible. It would be the Götterdämmerung, the Ragnarök, the final war – don't you think Man dreamed about that? The fables of Man are abundant with tales of cruel gods destroying Mankind, and every one of these gods are here on Earth with their celestial or subterranean armies – ghouls and trolls and angels and devils, Valkyries, gnomes, ghosts, witches – everything that two thousand generations of Man dreamed up in their most unspeakable, blackest dreams. Do you think that the goddess Nammu would have compassion with the sin of hybris? Or Zeus? Or Loki or Mithra or Seth or Horus or Demeter or any other of the thousands of omnipotent avenging gods of Man?' He shook his head, smiling tiredly. 'It is the curse of Man that he always creates his cruel gods to be omnipotent, while the good gods become small and powerless. There's no way out.'

He went around Monteyiller and stopped, leaning on the back of the chair. 'There's no way out,' he repeated.

Monteyiller stared vacantly at the distant wall. He felt the old fear rising again, the fear of the enemy that couldn't be fought; the old, old nightmare coming back again. The haven turned into a deadly trap. Finished.

'This is our world,' he said, 'and we'll have it, no matter what.'

'And what am I supposed to do about it?' The man's voice was calm, disinterested.

'Give us Earth!'

'I have already told you. I can't. And even if I could, I wouldn't.'

'We can't back out now,' Monteyiller said bitterly. 'We have to go on, whatever you say.'

'You will regret it,' the man said.

'Perhaps. But it might be worth the risk.' Monteyiller hesitated. Then he suddenly remembered. *Martha*.

'There was a woman on the first ship,' he said slowly. 'They were attacked, and she escaped. Where is she?'

'She's happy, as you would be happy if you let Earth have its will. She's in a world of her own making; she's loved by someone she thought dead. She's happy for the first time in many years, perhaps for the first time in her life. She needs Earth, the beings feel it, and they are doing anything that she asks. She'll never let you take her away.'

'Fantasies,' Monteyiller said. 'Drugs. Hallucinations. And she had a shock. You can't fool her forever. We'll get her back.'

The man said, 'You have been down the path to the kingdom of Death, you have met Heracles, you have met Alice, you have been in *Nautilus* and in a city of your own making.

You have been in Megacity. They weren't hallucinations, they were *real*. People have written about them, dreamed about them; they are yours if you want them. Earth wants you to have it. Your Martha was the first of you to find out. You will do the same.'

'We are speaking of different things,' Monteyiller said.

'Perhaps,' the man admitted.

'You could be destroyed.'

'Not by man.'

'If you turn against us,' Monteyiller said, 'we'll have to destroy you, one way or another.'

'You might find it harder than you think.'

'The beings that you talk about, they would help us, wouldn't they?'

'No doubt' – the man smiled coolly – 'but there would be a high price to pay for the help. I don't think you are that foolish, after all.'

Monteyiller rose from his chair. 'We'll find a way,' he said.

The man didn't answer. Monteyiller walked back to the door. It opened with a soft sighing sound before him. The space inside was black and hostile. He went in, feeling tired and hollow. When he looked back into the hall, the man had disappeared. He shrugged, and let the door close behind him. A pale light flickered in the darkness, and a moment later the door opened again. Megapolis had disappeared; there was soft grass outside, and a vague scent of flowers. There were fallen pillars, gleaming ghostly white in the moonlight. There were crickets. He stepped out from the dusk of the crumbling temple and found without surprise that he wasn't alone. He straightened and faced the girl who waited for him under the trees. She was rather small and slender, with long yellow hair falling down around a soft beautiful face. The body was that of a woman, but the eyes were those of a child, Alice. She was dressed in a pale blue shimmering garment that fell down to her feet. An ornamented golden belt girdled her slim waist. She was strangely enticing, desirable, and she stood unmovingly with one hand on her hip, gazing steadily at him.

16

In the Argine Dianeum: She disappeared in the shadows and returned a moment later.

'I brought you breakfast,' she said. 'You look tired.'

She lay bread and fruits before him, and poured red wine from an earthenware amphora.

He ate hungrily, conscious of her watchful eyes.

'What's your name?' she asked.

'Monteyiller. And you?'

'Nausikaa.'

'Only Nausikaa?'

She smiled. 'They used to call me "Nausikaa with the white arms". My father is Alkinoös, king of Phaiakia.'

'So I'm in royal company, then. Should I bow or something?'

She seated herself crosslegged before him.

'What are you doing here?'

He told her.

'The machine is of the same nature as everything else,' she said, looking away. 'It gives you the truth you want, not the truth that is.'

'But it said that it would resist us, that there would be wars. I don't want wars.'

She looked at him. 'Your ships are armed; you have a weapon at your thigh. Death hovers over you like a black cloud. Where Man goes, death follows him; you know that.'

Monteyiller looked thoughtfully at her. In the dancing light of the fire, she was beautiful. Time passed. She rose gracefully; the dress made a soft rustling sound. The fire painted her white arms red.

In the sanctum sanctorium and Ophelia: The air was dry and tinged with incense, and there was a shrine in the dusk, gleaming. Monteyiller glanced at it and frowned.

She said, 'Wants thou to lie in my lap?'

He said, 'Why not?'

'I mean, your head upon my lap.'

'Yes.'

'Do you think I meant country matters?'

He sighed. 'I think nothing.'

'That's a fair thought,' she said, 'to lie between maids' legs.'

She smiled, her lips red and moist. He could feel her heart beating through the gossamer folds of her dress. 'What is it?' he asked.

'Nothing.' She smiled.

'You're merry.'

'Why shouldn't I be merry, at such a place and such a time?' She leaned over him. 'Your ship is far away. You could stay here.'

He sat up. 'You're beautiful,' he said.

'Sweet Prince.' She laughed. 'I pray you to be silent, because my honesty admits no discourse to my beauty.'

She snuggled closer to him, her face hidden in his tunic.

'Tell me more,' she whispered.

She slept, golden hair streaming down over her face. She slept huddled up in fetal position, like a child. Her breathing was slow and even. The fire cast a golden shimmer over her skin. Monteyiller sat crouched before the shrine. He whistled between his teeth as he touched the gleaming dials. It was a rather curious shrine, far removed from the religious artifacts that could be expected in a place like this.

It was a subspace communicator.

The design was unfamiliar and archaic, and the texts on scales and dials were in some incredibly ancient language. But there was no mistaking what was in the transparent glassite dome, filled with myriads of oscillating pinpoints of

92

light, that crowned the gleaming cube: a direction-finder, and a highly advanced one too. The Confederation could not have matched it. It was a magnificent piece of machinery.

It was also brand-new.

The temple filled with the familiar low whine of the sub-space seeker-beam, abruptly ceasing as the communicator locked in on the fleet's frequency. The starry night in the dome dissolved into the face of a tired-looking officer with a cup held halfway to his mouth. He looked up, eyes widening.

'Captain Monteyiller!' he exclaimed. 'I –'

'The First Officer,' Monteyiller said, 'if you please.'

The officer's face dissolved into whirling iridescent mists that after a moment contracted and solidified into the image of a moustached, middle-aged man with dark, brooding eyes and a nervous twitch.

'Don't shout,' Monteyiller said amicably. 'You might disturb someone.'

The First Officer leaned closer to his visor screen. 'We've been calling you for the past ten hours – why haven't you kept in touch? Cat told me that –' He stopped and did something outside the communicator's field of vision. 'You aren't in the ship!' he said, returning to his former place. 'What's going on down there?' He was perspiring, Monteyiller observed, and he had obviously not shaved for some time. He felt a sudden pang of remorse for the man.

'I'm in some bloody temple somewhere,' he said, 'dedicated to the goddess Diana. And don't shout at me, because this place is a sanctuary and Diana disapproves violently of rough talk.' He paused to shoot a quick glance over his shoulder at the sleeping girl. Satisfied, he turned back to the communicator. 'What about Cat? Is she in the scoutship?'

'Well, yes. . . .'

'Tell Cat to lock herself in, if she hasn't done that yet, and to stay where she is until she gets picked up. We're moving in.'

'Sir –'

'I'm fine, thank you.' Monteyiller grinned wryly at the

astounded officer. 'Look, Stephen, we've got to do it sooner or later, and we're late as it is. This place isn't as innocent as it looks. *I* know. . . . what do you think they use this bloody communicator for? Scrambled eggs? They have an advanced civilization, Stephen, and that means trouble in capital letters. They've tried to break Cat and me down physically ever since we landed, and I just had a charming bribe in the form of a girl, in order to make me give in. If they don't want to contact us in a civilized way, we have to use other means.' He glanced down at his watch. 'Prepare for landing procedure, red alert with every bloody gun ready for immediate use. You have a position fix on me, haven't you?'

He didn't wait for the affirmative, but went on, 'You will follow plan B-three, three cruisers down to where I am and the rest of the fleet takes position in extended order, ready to move in if necessary. If you meet anything that acts hostilely, shoot. If you meet anything that might be hostile, shoot. If one of those bloody cathedrals or caverns or what-have-you starts to materialize around you, blast it apart and get out of it. Everything that acts funny is your goddamn enemy, no matter how improbable it seems. They look like hallucinations, but they aren't. I've been right in the middle of some of them. The plan goes into effect twenty minutes from now.'

He cast another quick glance at the sleeping girl. She murmured in her sleep. He hurried on, 'Get a position fix on Martha; you should be able to locate her by the stray radiation from her power-pack or something. We'll get her out from wherever she is, the first thing we do, and then we'll start talking business with the local authorities, whoever they might be. I've been kicked around enough; I don't intend to have any more of that.' He paused thoughtfully. 'And remember this is alien territory. It might be Earth, but don't let that fool you. Nothing, absolutely *nothing* is what you expect it to be. I've learned it the hard way; see to it that you don't have to do the same.'

There was a sound behind him, a soft rustle and bare feet approaching.

'Over,' he said, 'and out.'

In the end – the Medusa: As the image in the communicator's dome faded away, he caught her reflection in the curved glassite. The gargoyle face was distorted by hate, the hair was a mass of writhing snakes.

'You lied!' she screamed. 'You lied!' The piercing voice filled the temple as she came toward him.

'The Medusa,' Cat told him once, 'was one of the ancient Greeks' most imaginative inventions. It isn't just that she was ugly – she meant death. Those who saw her face were turned into stone. A real beauty, that one. The Greeks had a beastly imagination.'

He threw himself on the floor, covering his eyes with his hand and fired, fired until the temple blossomed with white dazzling death.

Later, careful to avoid looking at the scarred thing on the floor, he returned to the communicator. Whoever had put it there must have had reasons for it.

Never give the enemy an even break, Monteyiller thought grimly. *Better make it unusable.*

He unscrewed the back of the communicator. He stared into the opening, his mouth working wordlessly.

The machine was empty.

A Potemkin coulisse, a joke, an impossibility.

He rose slowly, staring out through the small door of the temple to the green landscape outside.

Everything here is out of some bloody book or other.
They're doing anything that she asks.
It gives you the truth that you want, not the truth that is.
Ali-
He looks at the scarred form on the floor.
-ce.
The forgotten writer who had envisaged the communicator hadn't bothered to describe the complicated machinery inside the gleaming shell; but, then, why should he? He had meant it

to work. In his novel, it did.

On Earth, where the fables ruled, it did.

Monteyiller aimed the disrupter at the communicator and fired. It crumpled and disappeared in a sphere of fire.

No machines were invincible. Not even in a writer's dreams.

Monteyiller left the temple, wondering if he really believed that.

17

Monteyiller stood at the edge of the pine forest, watching the last of the three Gargantuan ships descend to the ground. It loomed black and deadly before him, blotting out the morning sun, throwing a long black shadow far into the forest. Ports opened slowly in the hull; there were shouts and the sound of metal against metal; then men and vehicles began pouring out. Monteyiller watched it absently, failing to perceive the hard-drilled efficiency of the troops. They made a good show, and a lot of noise, but they were pitiably few. And none of them had been, to his knowledge, in actual combat before.

Cannon-fodder, he thought grimly. *Poor devils*.

Armed vehicles came rumbling down the embarkation ramp; three low-slung beetles of black metal slowly made their way toward the other two beetles that had emerged from the other ships. They left deep scars in the ground, winding between the groups of troopers and technical personnel that stood or sat in the grass, savoring the sights and smells of the morning. A group of veterans sat huddled together in a tight group at a distance, playing cards.

More vehicles came into view, bulky half-tracks that were built for exploration trips. Their usefulness in warfare could be disputed, but they were strong and reliable and had some light armaments. Eight of them came out in file and joined the beetles at a respectful distance. Farther away, four scout-ships hovered two feet over the ground. The expedition, a small-scale affair by any reckoning, was about ready to start. Monteyiller turned to Cat, who stood behind him in the shade of the trees, silently looking at the preparations.

'Well . . . what do you say about it?'

She glanced up at him. 'You're going out strong, aren't you?'

'Have to.' He stood broad-legged, hands on his hips, gazing approvingly at the activity. 'These . . . people are against us, have been ever since we came. I don't intend to give them the upper hand, now or ever. Martha is in that forest, probably surrounded by every devilish trick in the book and then some. They've got her, and they intend to keep her. Our only chance is to move in with so much force that they can't stop us, whatever they do. We're going to go in there, get her, and then back again. And after that . . .' He smiled. 'After that we'll start talking business with them.'

'At gun-point,' Cat said.

'We tried to contact them peacefully, didn't we?' He grimaced. 'And what good did that do us? Jocelyn is dead, torn to pieces by one of their creatures, and Martha is held as hostage. And the trip we were treated to – that one was not an accident. They knew bloody well what they did. First, intimidation, then violence, then bribery. They're cunning, the bastards. I've been playing along with them too long already, and it hasn't helped us a bit. Now we'll do this my way.'

Cat shrugged. 'I suppose you know what you're doing.'

Monteyiller was gazing through a field glass at a shimmering structure that rose up over the forest far away. Pale mist clung to shimmering towers, alternately hiding and exposing them to view. They looked like frozen fires in the red light of the morning sun. They were beautiful. They were growing.

'You bet,' he said.

It was a brisk, clear morning with a tinge of chill in the air. The fragrance of verdure and fermenting soil was mellow and rich, almost tangible. The column moved on, spearheaded by the five low-slung beetles. The pines fell wailingly to the ground as they pressed on. Sometimes they used the disrupters to burn them off, sometimes they just drove on, pushing them down. The result was the same. The column moved on. Behind it, a thirty-foot wide gash stretched through the forest all the way back to the ships, straight as an arrow. Soldiers sat on the roofs of the vehicles, cradling their guns.

He sat in one of the exploration half-tracks in the middle of the column. The window at his right was open; he had his elbow out, casually. He held a microphone in his left hand. In the beetle that led the column, another man held a similar microphone.

'Proceeding,' the receiver told him. 'No resistance.'

'It will come,' Monteyiller said. 'Watch out.'

He breathed deeply, savoring the taste of the violent, ancient spring. In the glades, blood-red flowers opened their cups in the warmth of the morning sun, and birds sang. Monteyiller observed it with something akin to awe; his own home planet was never like this. There, the seasons blended unnoticeably into each other, winter turning into summer like a tired whisper under a pale and motionless sky. Here the spring was like an explosion, a sudden scream of irresistible life, glowing in the chill of the morning air, blossoming and growing in a thousand shapes and smells from the eternal rich soil. It was wonder and magic, the never-ending triumph of Earth, deserted, cherished and wistfully remembered.

The column moved on.

On the roofs of the vehicles, the soldiers were swapping jokes. Overhead, the scoutships hovered, watching the column eat its way through the forest. Right in its path, the shimmering structure soared challenging toward the sky, shrouded in the whirling mists that only offered tantalizing glimpses of its crystalline beauty.

Monteyiller gazed up at the ships, squinting against the sun.

'Objective in sight,' the receiver said. 'Request further orders. We are now –'

The first wave of attackers swooped down from the blinding light of the sun. They fell like birds of prey, silent, swift and deadly. There were winged dragons, fire erupting from their jaws; there were flying horses, mounted by fair-haired women with the sun flashing in harnesses and shields and unsheathed swords; there was a drake, sailing the sky, its striped sail filled with wind as it bore down on the scoutships; there were chariots drawn by horses and dragons and goats; there were flying horses and flying men and giant birds. They came in thousands, a sky-full of improbabilities, so silently and swiftly that they were upon the ships before even the ships' cybernetic brains had time to react. Monteyiller watched in horror as a giant dragon fell down on one of the ships, clutched tight on its sleek hull and started to tear at the hull-plates. It disappeared in a ball of fire at a direct hit from one of the other ships, but within seconds another dragon rode on the ship. Beams of raw energy streamed out from the ships, slashing through the ranks of the attackers, almost casually reducing them to ash. The small ships darted to and fro among the creatures, spewing out death in all directions. They held their positions, but only just.

'Thorein!' Monteyiller whispered. 'I never thought –'

He was interrupted by a blinding flash, followed by a deep drawn-out roar. The half-track lurched violently and stopped. In the sudden silence, the sound of gunfire was plainly heard, coming nearer. The receiver crackled alive.

'Captain Monteyiller, sir?'

Monteyiller was staring out through the hastily closed window. The forest was alive with moving forms.

'Yes.'

'We are under fire, sir – massive bullets, it looks like. There's an army around us!'

The moving forms could be seen plainly now. They were men, dressed in uniforms. They swarmed out from the forest, shooting as they ran. The bullets ricocheted harmlessly from the vehicles.

Monteyiller said, 'What about our men?'

There was a short silence. Then, 'All accounted for, sir. They jumped into the trucks when the air attack started.' The voice paused. 'What are your orders, sir?' The voice came through over an increasing background noise of dull explosions and pattering gunfire. Monteyiller balled his fists, staring out through the window. Disrupter beams were raking

100

over the oncoming mass of attackers. Men were running around, screaming, their clothes burning. Trees caught fire and cast a flickering light into the shadows where more attackers waited behind primitive weapons, spitting out death against the column. The ground shook under the impact of bombs and grenades.

The loudspeaker said, 'They are bringing in artillery, sir.'

Monteyiller closed his eyes momentarily. 'I see.'

'Your orders, sir?'

Monteyiller looked down at his hands, flexing them, unflexing them.

'Sir . . . ?' the voice was insistent.

Monteyiller looked up. 'Retreat,' he muttered.

'Sir!'

'I said *retreat!* But we'll be back, don't worry!' He switched off the microphone and turned to Cat. 'A slight miscalculation on my part,' he said tightly. 'I never thought we'd run into anything like this. I have a lot to learn, it seems.' He glanced up at the sky, where the scoutships still were engaged in their dogfight against the airborne attackers. 'To think that one of the cruisers could have burned out everything in this bloody place before we went in . . . but I learn. I learn quick as hell when I have to.'

The front of the column was turning around, rumbling down alongside its tail of gleaming exploration half-tracks. At the same time, the violent attacks subsided, the steady hammering of artillery fire became more distant, and the attacking soldiers began slipping away into the shadows of the forest. When the first of the beetles passed Monteyiller's half-track, the forest was as quiet and peaceful as if the sudden murderous attack never had taken place. Only the scars left by the disrupters and the spreading fires were left to attest to the fighting. The two scoutships descended silently from the miraculously empty sky to pick up the defeated commander and the crew from his ruined vehicle.

Monteyiller halted in the airlock of the rescuing ship to cast a glance at the half-track. Its rear section was crushed as if by

101

a giant's fist. If whatever had struck it had hit a couple of feet nearer the front, Monteyiller wouldn't have lived to see the result. A near miss – or perhaps a warning: Next time will be final.

He looked up. Beyond the reach of his vehicles and guns, the shimmering towers soared gracefully up toward the sky, shrouded in pale luminescent mists. They seemed to mock him.

18

In the afternoon, the cruiser *Maedina* circled over the forest, at a respectful distance from the iridescent towers. In its wake, the forest shriveled and died. At the base, Monteyiller watched the changes that took place on the newly created wasteland.

Trenches appeared, winding over the smoking land. One line, two lines, three. Mist descended to the ground and solidified into miles of barbed wire. In the low scarred hills, gray bunkers squatted, surrounded by field-pieces of an incredibly archaic design. Men appeared, their uniforms gray, their helmets gray, their faces gray. They stood in groups, staring up at the circling cruiser. There were officers in bright blue uniforms, golden epaulets and swords. Some of them were mounted on horses, while men toiled, digging out entrenchments and shelters. Waves of heat rolled toward them from the burning forest. They mopped perspiration from their brows with gossamer handkerchiefs. They were cold, aloof – knights on a chessboard, waiting for the game to start.

In his command room aboard the flagship, the challenger looked up at the visor screen that covered the whole wall before him. The screen showed him the battlefield from above, in depth and full color. The enemy troops moved around like ants on a scarred bit of ground. They were strengthening their positions, awaiting his first move.

Monteyiller leaned back in his chair. He spoke into a microphone, watching the screen. At the edge of the wasteland, ten low-slung beetles rumbled forward from their hiding places in the shadows. Other vehicles followed, and soldiers. They were older than the ones who had gone on the first unsuccessful expedition; they walked crouched, with their weapons already aimed. Monteyiller had learned. This was no expedition. This was war.

The pawns advanced on the chessboard.

The night was alive with fire and the sounds of distant death. On the scarred plain, the chesspieces were locked in a war of positions, dug down into trenches facing each other's over a wide stretch of no-man's-land. There was barbed wire between them, and the smoking wrecks of armed vehicles. There were bodies of dead men, still clasping their weapons. They had been heroes, some of them, and cowards. In death, nothing told them apart.

Far beyond the lines, the challenger waited among his swarming soldiers, his machines and his plans; the shimmering towers scornfully soared up against the darkening sky.

Stalemate.

Monteyiller watched the screen in his command room. The chesspieces didn't move. There were occasional flashes of blinding white light, followed by a low distant rumble that could be heard through the hull of the ship. On smaller screens under the large one, there were images of soldiers gazing over the wasteland toward the enemy's trenches; waiting, watching, wondering. They all looked alike to Monteyiller. Soldiers always did. The loudspeakers spewed out the sounds of machine guns, artillery, disrupters, of men dying. Beneath the explosions and the screams of the disrupters was a low, steady droning, rising and falling.

'They've got aircraft,' Cat said.

She was reclining in a chair behind him, gazing with tired eyes at the large screen. Monteyiller shrugged indifferently.

'Toys. We could blast them out of the sky anytime.' He almost smiled. 'They're propeller-driven, can you imagine that? Old as hell; they're scraping the bottom of their resources.' He searched among the computer feed-outs that littered the table before him. 'The library identified some of them. Museum pieces, every one of them. Here. . . .' He

104

smiled absently. 'Fokkers, Messerschmitts, Spitfires, Dorniers. They're so ancient the central computer had to dig in the files for a couple of hours before it found even a passing reference to them. It's beautiful.'

One of the cameras picked up a low-flying aircraft that thundered over the treetops. Written in large, elaborate letters on the engine hood was: *Spirit of St. Louis*.

'Why don't you just go in and get it over with,' Cat said. 'You could do it anytime you wanted to.'

'In time,' Monteyiller said. 'I'm doing this my own way, taking it easy on them. They can't keep this up forever. I'm wearing them down. I have lots of time – they don't.'

'You're playing war,' Cat said. 'You always wanted to do this. It's nothing but a game to you.'

'I made a mistake at first,' Monteyiller said. 'I'm learning now. I'll get them down on their knees!'

'There are men dying out there.'

'I didn't start this, did I? I just want Martha and a settlement, that's all. They just have to stop fighting, and there won't be any war.'

'You could end this any time you wanted to,' Cat said. 'You just don't want to, because if they get crushed you won't be the big commander-in-chief any longer.'

'Spare me the psychoanalysis!' Monteyiller snapped. 'I'm doing this my way, you hear?'

Cat rose from her chair. 'I hear,' she said.

She walked out slowly from the command room, without looking back. Behind her, the loudspeakers spewed out the sounds of the battle. Monteyiller was talking into the microphone, ordering down another of the cruisers that circled around the planet. The enemy was bringing in reinforcements: long-range artillery, tanks, and a never-ending stream of soldiers in drab gray uniforms. Sleek fighters swooped down onto the hovering scoutships, spitting out fire.

The shimmering towers rose up from a small island of trees, surrounded by a rapidly widening wasteland where the machines of war rumbled toward each other. The ground heaved and shook, fireballs blossomed and died. All the time, more men, more machines poured out from the towers, an impossible, inexhaustible mass radiating out into the screaming inferno of the battlefield.

If Martha hadn't been in those towers, Monteyiller thought, *I would have blasted them away long ago. But they know I can't take that risk.* I'll go on like this forever, if I have to. *They can't go on, but I can. I have six cruisers waiting up there with reinforcements. I'll wear them down to dust before I'm finished. I won't even need the cruisers.*

But if I should and needed more –

I can get reinforcements from the Confederation. This world is ours. We keep what is ours. They could be here in a couple of weeks, if I needed them. I could ask for a thousand men, ten thousand, fifty thousand. We'll grind them down to nothing. I'll grind them down to nothing.

He stared at the screen, his lips drawn back in an almost painful grimace.

I'll never give up.

He spoke into the microphone. Cruisers landed and spewed out more supplies, more men, more machines. The night was alive with white, dazzling death. In the trenches, men died and were replaced. They all looked alike. They always did.

The challenger made a new move. The challenged counter-moved. Pawns moved out, according to the rules of the game.

Monteyiller looked up at the screen, contemplating a new move. The battle was spreading; perhaps he would have to move base back a mile or so. A perfectly reasonable move, in all respects.

Castling.

19

The battle went on, slowing down sometimes to a sporadic exchange of fire over the no-man's-land, then suddenly flaring up violent, continuous bombardment. The countryside was slashed and torn for miles around the shimmering towers that still rose mockingly from their surrounding island of unscathed trees. Men and equipment continued to pour out from the towers. The battlefield widened in concentric circles, like the ripples on water where a stone has been dropped. The roads were filled with fugitives. They passed the base in a never-ending column, pale and silent, carrying their meager belongings with them. Some of the guards at the perimeter of the base insisted they recognized some of the fugitives, that they were the same people walking by day after day, night after night. They were laughed at. All fugitives look alike. The uniform of fear and starvation is as de-individualizing as the uniform of the soldier.

There were also prisoners-of-war, sullen, bearded men who would say nothing except their rank and number. They were put together behind force-beams and did nothing but plot to escape. One group built a wooden horse for exercise, and used it to cover the opening of a subterranean passage that ended outside the prison compound. One prisoner escaped with the help of a female technician who had fallen in love with him. They were a constant source of trouble. Monteyiller delegated the headache to a subordinate, and forgot about it.

There were also allies.

They came for money or for glory or for hate, for the chance of looting or for reasons of their own. They came dressed in strange uniforms, carrying strange weapons or no weapons at all. They fought like devils and died as heroes in a war that they didn't even try to understand. They were mad, but useful.

Heracles came.

Monteyiller happened to be down at the gate of the base when he arrived at the head of an unlikely band of mercenaries. There were four men dressed in gaily colored, loose-fitting uniforms, knee-high boots, plumed hats and billowing cloaks, who called themselves the Three Musketeers. There was an old fat man who sat in a wheelchair and told everyone in sight that he was the good soldier Schweik and the enemy would be sorry if he ever got his hands on them. There was also a tall, brooding savage clad in a loincloth who spoke in grunts and coughs, and a black-clad masked man on a white horse who said nothing at all. And there was, of course, Heracles.

'Ho, little man!' he shouted, pushing the guards aside with a shove of his hand and walking up to Monteyiller, who had been gazing at the mercenaries with quiet resignation. 'I heard that you are going to start some little war or other, so I came to help you finish it!' He pounded Monteyiller on the back, laughing thunderously. 'Don't look so downcast, little man! Heracles is here, is he not? What do you want me to do, little man?'

Monteyiller waved away the guards. He said, 'Didn't you have a labor to do for that king of yours?'

'Aye.' Heracles grinned. 'I have done that one – and one extra besides, one that the king didn't like! That's why I had to leave you so sudden; he sent his jackal after me to remind me of the hell-hound Cerberus that I was supposed to fetch for him. Now it's done and over with, and here I am. Now, what do you want me to do?'

'One of us is imprisoned in those towers over there,' Monteyiller said. 'A woman. We want her out.'

'You are taking too much trouble for a woman,' Heracles said. 'No woman is worth fighting for, believe me. Anyway' –

he grinned – 'Heracles has seen wars before; he knows a pretext when he sees one. Did I tell you about Helen of Troy and the accursed war they started for her sake? "Just to liberate her, nothing else," they said. The liars! Never has an army so much as lifted a foot for a fair maiden's sake unless she's been sitting on a mountain of gold. I'll help you, little man!' He laughed joyously, slapping his thigh with an enormous hand.

They walked up toward the flagship. Monteyiller said, 'We want what is ours, nothing else. If they refuse to give it to us, we'll take it. That's all there is to it.'

'That's all there is to any war.' Heracles grinned. 'Same humility, same unselfishness, same liberation, same corpses, same looting, same raping, same death. I know about wars.' He glanced at Monteyiller. 'And this will be a long and beautiful one. They won't give her up, I know them.'

'I have time,' Monteyiller said.

'And I will help you!' Heracles shouted. 'By Zeus, I will! I'm a man of peace at heart, anyone knows that, but never has Heracles been known to skulk away from a fight! You are a man of my taste, little man,' he roared, slapping Monteyiller's back. 'We'll show them, the swine! We'll cut them to pieces! I know this place, little man; with me beside you there'll be sweet grapes of victory waiting for us, you can be sure of that!' He grinned happily down at Monteyiller. 'Now, what I would suggest at the moment would be to send some of your soldiers down to a small town not far from here – it's hardly more than a village, actually – and seize it. Won't be any trouble at all, you'd know how to do it. The people in that town are friends of Alice, see? And you wouldn't want to have her friends that close to you, would you? It would only cause you trouble in the future, it would. When you have that, I have a wonderful plan for you, a magnificent plan, a plan that only Heracles could make.'

Cat sat in the canteen of the flagship, staring up at the small visor screen. There was a cup of pseudo-coffee on the table before her, untouched. On the screen, the battle was rapidly spreading out beyond its original boundaries. Reinforcements were pouring in from all around Earth, to Monteyiller's army as well as to the enemy's. Soon there would be reinforcements from the Confederation as well. The message was on its way, telling of the first opposition the Confederation had met since it had been formed. With those forces, Supreme Commander Monteyiller could fight forever if he had to.

She stared up at the screen where the fighting went on and on and on.

He would.

Monteyiller had a cot set up in the command room. He seldom left the room now. He was totally occupied with his game of chess, moving pawns, bishops and knights over the rapidly growing chessboard, seeking openings, making plans, anticipating the opposing player's moves. It was a war of mind against mind, far above the heads of the chesspieces. The game of war made him jubilant, excited, joyous.

For the first time in his life, Monteyiller was completely happy.

20

The reinforcements from the Confederation arrived. There
were twenty-two cruisers, screaming down from space, soldiers, cannons, beetles, equipment. They came from the blue
sky in wave after wave, spewing out death, licking the clouds
with tongues of fire, roaring over the sleeping plains, the
rolling seas, the high mountains. The destruction was satis-
factory; so was the resistance. Castles changed themselves
into launching sites; ancient towers climbed up toward the
sky, changing into sleek metal-glittering rockets on their way;
the ground opened and strange creatures appeared, riding the
sky on moonbeams and fire. There was death, destruction
and glory; more than enough for anyone. The cruisers fought
the attackers, annihilated them, turning the ground into a
burning, flowing hell. Then they moved on to the battlefield
and the eternal stalemate.

Behind them, the land was healing. The castles reappeared,
villages grew up, cities spread over the countryside. There
was no mark, no scar left of the terrible destruction. It was all
set up for a new, beautiful victory.

In a small, sunlit glade, Martha lay in the grass close to
someone who could have been Jocelyn but was not. There
was eternal peace, far away from the war games of others'
minds. Martha was quiet and romantic. There was a small
house set in among the trees. A cottage. A summer-house. A
palace. She hadn't decided yet. For the first time in her life,
Martha was completely happy.

Monteyiller watched the war game on the visor screen in

the command room. It was still a limited war, concentrated around the unattainable towers. He gained a little bit here, lost a little bit there. The enemy fought hard and well. A worthy opponent.

I'm winning, he thought. *Slowly but surely, I'm winning*.

As the days turned into weeks and the weeks into months, he sometimes wondered if he'd made any headway at all, if he ever would win the game of chess, or if he actually might lose it. But then he always made a brilliant move, a small victory, a spearhead into the enemy's territory. He was happy again.

On a low hill overlooking the base, Alice stood, the multi-colored ball at her feet, looking out over the rolling hills. The fierce battle was hardly a dent in the immense expanse stretching out before her. Somewhere, a sleek metal body blasted away from a hidden missile site and climbed up toward the sky, trailing bright fire. It was destroyed in a counter-move by Monteyiller before it even started to fall down to its target.

Alice stood motionless, looking up at the fireball. She started to dissolve, changing into someone else: to Juliet of Verona, with her hair streaming in the wind and a small sharp-edged dagger in her hands; to Demeter Chamyne, clad in an appealing earth-colored dress; to Rhea, to Numbakulla, to Astarte. She towered terrifyingly dark over the land until she changed again, to a radiant pale being, a small slender woman with large dark eyes called Beatrice Portinari, seen through an entranced poet's eyes. Then she was Alice again. She pouted childishly, and the long yellow hair fell down over her shoulders. Far away, the battle went on and on. She didn't see it. She clasped her hands behind her back, stretched her arms till the joints cracked. She raised herself on the tips of her toes. The starry sky arched above her, clear and scintillating. She looked up at the darkening sky from which Man was returning to his deserted dreams.